# THE UNFORGIVABLE

# By Judy Serventi

# PROLOGUE
## Lost

Does it bother me when people arrogantly look at me pulling my wheelie bag? Not really. At least I am not pushing a shopping cart through the streets. Well, not yet, I have no desire to collect stuff. Not anymore. I am too old, too bitter, and too angry.

Yes, I am homeless. If that's the stigma I must carry with me, so let it be. Stare at me, with your disquieting looks. I am past being concerned by what you think or see. I wasn't always like this. My journey here could have been different, but it wasn't. We are taught from an early age to avoid weird looking adults and I suppose I do look strange. I am wearing a dirty coat because I sleep on the floor, and my face is dirty and my hair scruffy, a far cry from my twice weekly visits to the beauty salon to have my hair and nails seen to. My body bends forward as I pull my bag, not from the weight in it, but for the fact that I would rather look down so I don't trip over something. It's amazing how many potholes there are on the streets and byways.

I have only one main problem each day and that is to find somewhere to sleep. I am weary of the 'shelters'. They ask too many questions, and I am worried about losing my wheelie. This is what I have left, all that matters to me at this present time.

I could go to a cheap rooming house or a small motel, but they are fraught with danger. Some churches still leave their doors open at night so they have become my first choice. I can arrive late and leave early. Sometimes I go in during the day to talk out loud to the statues, to ask questions that usual follow the same narrative – "Why me?" or "I didn't deserve this?" Then I realize that self-pity will not help me survive.

I was humiliated, disgraced, but not dishonest. I lived by the rules; it was not my fault. Fate put me here and now my destiny is in my hands. I hope I can stay strong in mind and body to end this nightmare. I believe in me. My quandary is what matters to me most now – a life not lived or a life mistakenly lived?

I thank my parents for giving me strong healthy genes. The system can't take that away from me. I am grateful I don't require medication; just the bare minimum of needs will see me through. Moving to Florida was at least one good decision we made. Yes, there was once a person who gave me much love, much comfort, much solace. I didn't appreciate how lucky I was back then. It wasn't something I ever had time to think about. Life was good. We laughed together, we fought together, and we accepted and forgave each other and compromised. Nobody could have foreseen what was to come.

I have to sit on this bench for a while and contemplate my next move, but my eyes are drawn to a young lady who is stopped at the red light. Her manicured hands grip the steering wheel and her head of long blond hair swings from side to side as she listens to the music coming from the speakers of her slick new car.

I identified with her young frivolous nature. Her pleasure and delight with the moment. She smiled at me before pulling away with a perky nod of her head, which I didn't respond to. My mind was wandering back to a time when I was happy with my hectic lifestyle, and unconcerned about things I couldn't fix.

# Chapter 1
# February 14th 1965

George and I always had breakfast together; it was something we just did back then. We had been married only a year and we lightheartedly exchanged Valentine cards and laughed aloud at the incongruity of the words. Living together wasn't always a bed of roses. We were both still exerting our own wishes and choices on each other.

Compromise was still an attitude neither of us was comfortable with We were headstrong youthful people. The 60's movement of freedom of expression, and opportunity, especially for women, had maybe affected my standpoint. I was blatantly refusing to be the underling, and sometimes the outcome of my attitude was misconstrued. Maybe, not what I intended, but we overcame these situations with love and laughter. I think we both respected the candidness and willingness to speak our minds instead of harboring the grudge.

We had waited a long time before we were ready for marriage. Our careers had been paramount. Justifying who we were, climbing the work ladder, and establishing superiority in the workplace had come before romance and dating for us both. It was unusual at that time to wait until you were over thirty, but I was used to being on my own, and actually dismissed the idea of being a lonely spinster. I enjoyed my independence; that was, until I met George.

George worked in the financial world and I sold real estate. We both were happy in our field of work, and the lucrative reward we saw helped fuel our tastes for the finer things in life.

I had found this house – a real steal – in a good area and George, of course knew how to raise the finance. We settled in straight away, and never thought it was a lucky situation to be in at that time in our lives. We thought it was due to our ability to work the situation to our own advantage, so we grew smug in our accomplishments.

The situation of our house in an affluent neighborhood brought us new friends with similar aspirations. George bragged along with our neighbors about their new purchases. They all had a thirst for material things. Only the very best was tolerated in this myopic world.

We often ate dinner out, and experimented with the food and wine of different countries. This led to us wanting to visit these places, and try the cuisine first hand. Over the next few years this is how we molded our lives. We both worked long hours. George was required to work late numerous weekday evenings, on account of the time differences in International Banks. I worked many weekends at 'open houses'. Therefore, we both thought we were entitled to splurge when it came to vacations.

Dinner parties were another of our indulgencies. Attending the ones our neighbors invited us to, or when we tried to outclass them with our choices of food and wine. George was meticulous in choosing the right wine with the food we were serving. He really felt he was a wine connoisseur because of our travels. He would spew out the joys of his wine choice of the evening, as he swirled his glass in the air, purposely telling the guests to sip, and not slurp the nectar.

I honestly thought he looked rather foolish, but our company would always be convinced, and obeyed his request to follow his actions with their wine glasses. If anything, George was good at influencing people, and persuading them he knew everything there was to know on certain subjects. He was a good talker, but not a good listener. It had been a good dinner party in George's eyes if he had "held fort" during most of the evening.

Sometimes he would ask colleagues from his work to join us, but they were always the minor employees, rather than his contemporaries in the office, so he could impress them. When I pointed this out to him, he would get very angry, and tell me to ask my colleagues to come to dinner.

Now that was not going to happen. As far as I was concerned my work place, and my home were two entirely different areas of my life. I truly liked it that way. I was a very private person. I learned after my parents died never to wear my heart on my sleeve. In fact I was not a very sociable person. I was cautiously friendly and not very forthcoming with my personal life. I would be very affable with our guests, but I was always pleased to see them go. That is not to say I am a weak person, I can be as strong and demanding as George if it is something I need to do. My tasks at work were never problems to me, but only challenges I needed to overcome.

George and I were opposites, but we fulfilled each other. We both were satisfied in our marriage, and neither of us strayed in our relationship that I was certain of. We were enjoying our hard earned gains. Spending on the necessities we thought were important gave us mutual pleasure. Nevertheless, this spiral of self-gratitude was slowly fading.

We had no close family to share our lives with. We heard small children in the neighborhood laughing and playing together, and their parents proudly gushing about their off- springs' achievements. Now it was our turn to be jealous. The pang of parenthood was prodding us for consideration.

We decided to start a family. To some people this would be an accident of pleasure or, a success after years of trying, but not so for George and me. This had to be a calculated objective. We scanned the web for indications of what we could expect with this goal. George looked at the figures for the extra expense for this added family member, both now, and into the future. I read everything I could about pregnancy, the good, the bad, and the ugly. Some would tell us we were never going to realize the full impact that a baby would have on us until it happened. However, this train of thought was not in our heads. Good planning was paramount in avoiding problems. This was how we had become successful in our working lives and in our marriage. Preparation for the unexpected needed to be addressed beforehand, and then it was not a big matter to deal with later.

Once our calculations and expectations had been mutually agreed upon, then the timing had to coincide with our work schedules. The best time to ovulate was not always in tune with our work calendar, and sometimes we were not in the same frame of mind. Tiredness and frustration also came into play. Finally, it miraculously happened. I was pregnant and once more we both patted ourselves on the back for a job well done.

I must say I was not happy about how I looked, and how I felt. We had decided that I should keep working as long as possible, and as George pointed out, sitting at a computer was not strenuous work, and the outside visits could be delegated.

I had to start using our second bathroom due to the onslaught of recurrences of me being sick. My nausea upset me, and it affected George's stomach too, because he couldn't stand the smell. I fully understood his attitude as I also could not clean the effected area. The outcome was the first change to George's calculations – we had to get a cleaner. It was either swallow the extra expense or, contend with the dirty bathroom, both of which George was not thrilled with. He got past it, and learnt to accept this extravagance when he discovered that most of our neighbors already had this excessiveness in their homes.

I have to say that I didn't realize at that time that George was turning into a snob. It was just the way we lived. Our neighbors and associates were all like-minded individuals who drew us into their world and applauded our ambitious behavior. It was the norm. George's parents had died before I met him so I had no idea if it was an inherited trait or not. My parents died in a plane crash when I was in University and both of us had no siblings so, sharing my hopes and fears were restricted to those around me.

I was glad to have a cleaner in the house. June was a good listener as well as an impeccable cleaner. As the months went by I found myself not wanting to leave the house. The sickness hadn't diminished after the first three months, as my research informed me it should, and so June took on more and more responsibilities like shopping, doing laundry, and accompanying me to my Doctor's appointments. This again meant a re-evaluation of the budget, but was deemed a necessary adjustment for us both.

Carrying a child brought emotional as well as financial consequences. I missed my Mother immensely as I did my Dad's common sense attitude. I wanted her to tell me what to expect and endure, and not rely on a screen full of information. I wanted her Motherly advice, and her tender understanding as only a Mother knows. My maudlin attitude was lost on George, but thankfully, June understood and supported me through the trauma.

I sat in the Doctor's office listening fearfully to the tales from the other Mothers. June tried to divert me from the conversations, but I was eager to hear all, even though it was scaring me to bits. My good imagination was adding to the explanations. I was getting enormous in size, and I could not fathom how this child could get out of my body. More and more I was leaning towards a C-Section rather than the natural way.

I discussed this with my Gynecologist, but was told that would only be done if really necessary, and anyway I was a healthy young woman who would get used to giving birth. I was definitely unhappy with that comment. I was certainly not enjoying this experience, and was not looking forward to repeating it.

June told me from her own personal experience that the feeling of holding your baby after the birth made the painful past disappear in minutes. She told me it was such a wonderful sensation, and worth every pang of pain. I tried to hold on to that thought during the next few weeks.

As my due date came nearer I felt more and more isolated and lonely in our big house. George never came home before 8p.m. so the days seemed long. I decided to stop work when I reached my 3rd trimester, as I was still vomiting, plus I always felt drained and exhausted. Even if I took a nap in the afternoon, by the time George came home I was ready to go to bed again. As a result, I was terrible company; however, on this matter he was very considerate, and if I did go off to bed early he would go into his office to do yet more work.

This arrangement suited us both at that time. June fixed dinner before she left, because even a cooking smell would leave me running for the bathroom. She was my mainstay, my support for everything. She was irreplaceable in my eyes, and I could not have coped without her. Back then I could not understand how pregnant women who couldn't afford to have paid help managed. Conversely, this was not a subject I needed to discuss with George; of late he had been giving June regular extra bonuses in her wage with no bother at all. Recently he had been buying more and more 'stuff' and giving me flowers for no apparent reason. I wondered if my pregnancy was making him feel guilty.

This matter caused me to question our financial situation with him one evening. I began by asking if the extra work he was doing was because we only had one income coming in. His answer to me was too incredible and hard to believe. It didn't seem to fit with the careful, cautious George I had married.

My vigilant husband was going into business. He was working on setting up his own financial establishment. He remarked that he was tired of putting all his ideas and efforts into a company that didn't appreciate him. Moreover, he was going to use his work contacts for his own ends.

I was speechless, and my muddled mind did not comprehend this information. I knew he was talking to me because his animated face, and gestures were directed towards me, but nothing made sense.

I put up my hand, and went towards him pleading with him to stop for a minute. He was sitting at his office desk, but stood up and was walking towards me. I met him and wrapped my bulging shape around him, and for some unknown reason I began to cry,

George soothed me and told me there was another time and place to discuss this subject, so I should go to bed.

"I don't want you to worry about anything at the moment. You are not ready to discuss this matter, and indeed, you needn't be concerned. I am still working for the Company, and this sideline of mine has not come to fruition yet. So let's just concentrate on you and our baby."

He said this as he patted my stomach, and kissed my forehead. His reassurances were all I needed that evening. I was worn out from doing nothing, and I knew I would go to sleep as soon as my head hit the pillow, which was the case.

In the morning I awoke and turned my heavy body, expecting to see George. It was Saturday, and that usually meant George would sleep late, and enjoy the extra time in bed.

His side was empty, so I thought it must be me who was sleeping late. I checked the clock, which was lit up showing me the time clearly. It was 6.45a.m.

I listened to hear if he was in our bathroom, but that wasn't the case. I struggled to ease myself out of bed. This was yet another chore that was proving to be a task and a feat in itself. To achieve this simple undertaking, for me, often took many maneuvers that left me breathless. Again I wondered how other Mothers managed; I was feeling totally inadequate to handle this simple assignment of being pregnant.

Finally, I succeeded; I pulled a robe around me and went to find my husband. I heard him in the study talking on his cell. He was obviously talking business, so I went to the kitchen to make a pot of coffee, thinking he must be dealing with one of his International clients. I went to get the newspaper from the front door, and returned to the kitchen just as the percolator was finishing. I decided to take some coffee through to George without questioning him on his early rise. As I went through the door he abruptly finished his call, well, at least, that is what it seemed to me. However, I smiled at him, and put the coffee down on his desk, tentatively saying,

"Thought you would like this dear, would you like some toast?"

He moved the papers from near the coffee mug angrily answering.

"Be careful, these are important, I don't want anything spilt over them."
After further shuffling of the papers, he continued. "You are rather clumsy these days. Thanks, but I am rather busy at the moment I'll eat later. You go ahead and have something to eat.

You are eating for two now", he added with a conceited smile.

Before I could break into tears I left him dialing another number, obviously continuing his important calls.

I went to the kitchen, poured my coffee, and decided to read the newspaper to read about other folk's troubles instead of woefully accepting mine. George didn't join me for breakfast, nor did he emerge for lunch. Luckily I had June to talk to, and hear about her family squabbles which she just scoffed at, and always saw the amusing side to them.

June was the only person I felt at ease talking to. She listened intently when I confided my fears and worries I had about the birth. My own Doctor, my Gynecologist, and the nurses in these offices seemed to make fun of my questions. This might have been my fantasy as I listened to their rationalizations, but nothing they said made me feel comfortable.

"That's what you get when you go to these expensive private medical centers, dear." June said, after I mentioned my unease to her. "You should come to my Pre-natal Clinic. They have done me right through all five of my kids. It's not a fancy place, but they take medical insurance with a small co-payment. Thank goodness my Fred gets medical cover for us all with his job. I've been to your place with you, and seen your lot; they're only interested in your money, dear. The more you visit the more money they get!"

I had to smile at her response, she did know both places, and was the only person I knew who could compare them.

I decided I must talk to George to get his reaction to my dilemma, but getting him away from his office was not an easy task. If I went in with a drink or something to eat for him, he would tell me to leave it in the kitchen, and he would microwave it later. When later came, I was usually in bed or at my numerous doctor's appointments

One time we did manage to be in the kitchen at the same time, and I brought up the subject of not feeling comfortable with the medical personnel I was seeing. His reply -

"Darling if you want to change then you must decide. At this time you deserve the very best, but really I would not know where to start, and I frankly have not the time to research this situation. I'm sure you have people you can ask, it really is a woman's state of affairs."

With that unhelpful retort George left the kitchen with his plate of food, nonetheless first drinking his glass of wine in one gulp – I suppose to avoid it spilling on his precious papers, if he had taken it through.

The next day I spoke to June about her clinic, and decided to give it a try. I did not mention this to George, as he obviously did not wish to know.

The Pre-natal clinic was inside our local hospital, and catered for a large urban population. Needless to say it was a big facility with a large waiting room. June directed me to a window where a receptionist asked if I was a new patient, and if so, could I fill in the necessary paper work that she handed to me on a clipboard, before she quickly closed the window.

I looked around the large room, and saw June waving to me at the back where she had fortunately found two seats unoccupied. I had been used to a secretary doing this for me so, the large amount of questions were tedious and boring.

"Just answer what you can," said June recognizing I was having problems. "Put the important stuff down that you do know the answer to. They will ask you for your driving license, and insurance card when you take this back."

Sure enough that's what happened, and the clerk told me she would call me when it was my turn. As I turned to walk away she called me back, and abruptly asked if I had signed in with my appointment time. Then she pointed to another clipboard that was on the small counter where I put my name at the bottom of the list.

The room had an eerie atmosphere. It was quiet, with only whispered conversations between the pregnant ladies and their companions taking place. Occasionally this silence was interrupted by a nurse shouting a name. Very different from my private clinic with the small intimate sitting room where you saw the same people on each visit. I got to know their names along with all their confidential details of past pregnancies, and sex problems with their husbands. Most of it I didn't want to be acquainted with. Their drivers or companions had to wait in a different space so the large comfortable chairs occupied only 5 or 6 women.

Two hours later I still had not been called, and I was ready to leave, but June insisted I shouldn't go yet, as there were very few people left in the waiting room my turn would soon come. She went to the vending machine to get us both a drink, and while she was away my name was called.

The Doctor was an elderly man who had a nice bedside manner, but looked slightly weary from his heavy workload. His nurse did the usual height, weight and blood pressure test while the Doctor seemed to be catching up with his notes. His questions to me were mostly about why I hadn't been to the clinic before now. I lied and told him I had just moved into the area, but I had been seeing a gynecologist who had been happy about my progress. He asked me if I had any questions or concerns, and that was certainly the case, for me. I was eager to explain my fears of child-birth which he responded in a matter of fact way,

"That is normal for first time Mothers, don't fret about it. Just relax, and the reward will be your compensation when you have a little child in your arms."

He gave me a brief examination and then asked the nurse to schedule me for an ultrasound the following week.

I let the nurse do this, even though I knew I was not going to carry out the appointment. I didn't want June to be offended, but I had to admit to her later that I was not really happy with uncomfortable chairs, the atmosphere, and the long waiting time. Her answer was straight and to the point,

"Well, some of us have no choice in the matter, but now you do have this option," she said this with a wry look on her face followed by a smile. I smiled back and the subject was closed.

# Chapter 2
# Looking For Answers

I was in my 3rd trimester and was round about 31weeks when I really felt unusually weak. I couldn't keep my food down, and was still frequently vomiting. June was the only person around that day, and she was extremely anxious. She asked if I had any pain or discomfort in my groin which was very important if that was the case, and it meant we had to get to clinic immediately – whichever clinic I wished, but we must go now.

I told her I had terrific backache, and felt I could not hold my bladder from leaking. She grabbed my car keys, scuttled me into my Mercedes, and told me she would drive.

We went to my private clinic, where we valet parked. Then the valet called for a wheelchair, and took me inside to reception. I caught hold of June, and asked her to let George know where I was. Everything was going fast, but I was too disorientated to understand what was happening, although everybody seemed to know my name, and were consoling me that the pain would be taken care of.

I remember being put into a bed, and then a lot of commotion and turmoil around me. After that the next few hours were just a blur. I had a vague impression of seeing doctors and nurses I recognized, but then nothing.

I don't know how much time had gone by, but my pain had left my body. In fact, I also knew that the baby had left my body. I touched my stomach to confirm the truth; however, my hand was joined by George's.

"You must rest," he said in a whisper. "You have gone through a lot and I know we will be back to normal very soon. There is nothing for you to worry about. When you are strong enough we will travel to Europe, I know that's your favorite place."

"But George we can't take the baby overseas so soon. I didn't go to full term so...George, why are you looking at me in that funny way, where is my baby? Let me see my baby!" I yelled.

He continued to pat my hand that was still on my stomach as he shook his head, but he didn't answer. I thought I saw a tear drop from his bent head on to our hands. I had never seen emotion like this from him.

"George did I lose the baby? Did I do something wrong? Was it my fault? I'm sorry; I am a failure for you. I tried. I really did try." I sobbed.

I could not believe I was unsuccessful in something that was so commonplace, so routine for many women. Even June could accomplish this task five times.

George tried to comfort me in his matter of fact way.
"Maybe it was meant to be like this for us. When I think about it I don't think I would have made a good Father, I haven't a great deal of patience to play with children, and at the moment I have a lot going on."

I looked into his face, and saw that his grief had been short lived. I could sense he had more essential things to do than sit at my side. He was diverting his attention to the clock on the wall, and shifting around on the bedside chair in an uncomfortable posture.

"You don't need to hang around here, I am feeling rather sleepy. I will be fine." I lied.

That was obviously what he was hoping for, because he stood up quickly, kissed me on the forehead, and said he would see me later in the evening. I was not sleepy, I needed to speak to someone and get to know the truth about my premature birth. I rang for some attention, which came immediately, in the form of my doctor and a nurse.

I started, hesitantly with my eyes full of tears, looking into the face of my doctor.

"Did I lose my baby?"

He came closer to by bed and looked down at me nodding his head. He was going to speak, but I interrupted.

"Why? Could I have prevented this happening? Should I have done more?

"First and foremost you are not to blame," he answered sternly. "Your baby was stillborn; many factors could have been the cause of your pre-term birth. You are, if you don't mind me saying, rather petite and your husband is tall and well-built. Your baby, who was a boy, by the way, seemed to inherit his father's genes. Maybe your age could be a contributing factor. Or the baby could have died for some reason in your womb. We could do an autopsy if you want."

"No. Oh! Oh! No." I blurted out. "I don't even know if I want to see the baby."

"It is for you to decide. I will give your husband the death certificate, and then I am sure he will make the arrangements from there. You need to stay here for a little longer so we can build up your strength," was his hasty reply.

For the next few days I stayed in the hospital doing a lot of sleeping. George was very busy, so he said, but I really didn't want to talk to anybody. The private room gave me all I needed at that time; however, George decided after four full days, I should try to get back to normal. He didn't say if this decision was financially based or if he missed me. I suspected that my husband liked normality in his home life, so it was that I returned.

There were bunches of flowers everywhere and I knew June had been diligently cleaning to make my homecoming pleasant. Apparently, the flowers were from neighbors, work colleagues as well as my husband. To me it looked like a funeral parlor, which prompted the question.

"What are we going to do with our son? Giving him no time to answer I continued, "I want a quiet cremation and then we can bring home the urn until we can decide later what to do with his ashes."

"Whatever you wish, that is fine with me. I will make those arrangements first thing tomorrow," he replied in a sympathetic manner.

At that moment I wanted him to hug me, but instead he called June, who was in the kitchen, to bring us some hot tea, which June did straight away - she always anticipated actions before they were called for. It was uncanny, but kind. When she had put the tray down I stood up and gave her the embrace I needed, and thanked her for everything she had done for me. My husband was embarrassed so he looked down to his teacup and drank.

There was a long silence until George remarked he had something to tell me.

"I've decided to go ahead and form my own company; I think I discussed it with you a few months ago?"

"Well, we didn't actually discuss it; you told me that was your intention." I interrupted

He haughtily continued. "Nevertheless I have indeed gone ahead with this matter since you were somewhat pre-occupied with your,….err excuse me, our, other important issues."

"George why are you being so abrasive with me? If you feel you want to make a career change, and you know you can do it, then I would be the last person to interfere with your choice. We have never stopped each other from following their dreams. My dream, no, our dream, didn't work out, but that shouldn't stop you from pursuing your vision. If that's what you really want, then you have my support."

He finally came towards me and gave me the cuddle I had been waiting for. He squeezed me tight, kissed me and said,

"You are the best. I'm sorry for my attitude, but I was afraid you would not want me to leave the security of having a dependable income, especially just now. Believe me; I will make it work for us. I have only been working on my ideas part-time, and I have seen a substantial increase in returns. So much so, I have obtained an office in downtown, and I am looking to hire a commercial lawyer to work with me. I also need you to be by my side, in the social commitments I must make. Not just yet, but as soon as you feel ready for the undertaking. Would you do this for me?"

I smiled and replied, "I am your wife, your confidant, your supporter. I am the only person who can carry out that position in the company."

# Chapter 3
# Moving Forward

The cremation of our son took place quietly, and reverently, with just the two of us in attendance. I brought home the small urn, and put it discreetly at the back of my closet. I was not sure what I wanted to do with the ashes, time would tell, and then I would act accordingly.

I knew I had to occupy myself, and not dwell in the past. George told me he would involve me in his business when he had finished the preliminary formation of his company. Each day he was occupied in registrations, hiring people, renting office furniture, and I can only guess there would be a lot of scheduling, preparation and setting up of contacts. He worked tirelessly, but energetically seeking the perfection George liked, assiduously dealing with every small detail.

I offered to lend a hand, but my enthusiasm was unwanted.

"I have a place for you, my dear, and it is not in the office. Go to the beauty salon, or to the shopping mall. I want you to be ready when our social activities begin. I will make sure there is enough in our personal account to cover your expenses."

Then he finished his breakfast quickly, and with a big smile on his face, he jauntily stepped to the front door, put on his coat, picked up his briefcase and opened the front door. Subsequently, with his mind obviously racing ahead, he turned in my direction and blew me a kiss.

I returned to my breakfast, but discarded the plate. I held my coffee mug in both hands, and looked down into the frothy liquid. My mind was blank. I had no thoughts, no purpose, nowhere to go and nothing to do. Trying to snap out of my downward spiral I picked up the newspaper, which was on the table, urging my brain to be positive, and alert, instead of being gloomy and pitiful.

Not long afterwards, cheerful June came into the kitchen, apologizing for being late and spelling out all the problems she had faced that morning, trying to get all five of her children out of bed, and into the school building. A daunting task that I couldn't even imagine taking on.

However, as she loaded the dishwasher, her narrative regarding each of her children, and their mischievous ways turned out to be a farcical and nonsensical interlude of hilarity, and delight for me. Her stories were the therapy I needed. Her daily tasks were reflected as trivial chores that could be interpreted as enjoyable. June was the most positive person I had ever been in contact with. I was resolute at that time to try to be like her. Who would have thought that my household help could be my role model?

She had the ability to do two things at once with ease and precision. Her conversations of events in her life were never dull, and her chores for me never lacked in thoroughness. That morning I didn't miss the opportunity of telling her how I appreciated her in my life, to which she replied,

"You know what's wrong with you? You are depressed. But don't think you are unique; the medical folks have named it. They call it postnatal depression, or postpartum depression, or simply P.P.D. My sister had it bad after her miscarriage, and many women I know got it. I even had this condition after my first. I'm no doctor, but I've been around Mothers and babies for a good few years, and I can see it in you right now."

"I feel so helpless, June. I blame myself for not being capable of having a healthy baby. I imagine how wonderful life would be with a baby to love and to nurture. I don't want to go out and see

Mothers pushing strollers or see children playing outside. I haven't even been for my check-up at the clinic in case I meet the women who have been successful."

She came towards me as I sat at the kitchen table, and gently put her large round hands on my shoulders, squeezing with a tender touch. In a soft soothing voice she continued,

"You have to know that this anxiety you feel, can and will go away. It takes a little time and effort. Believe me you can make it happen. Your husband's pretty busy at this time, and I suppose you haven't said anything to him anyhow. You are not a useless person. You have a great many gifts you can share. Now is your chance to be yourself, be a good citizen and a good wife."

She turned to the sink, wiping her hands on her apron, apparently cleaning the nervousness from them.

"I probably have no right to push my analysis on you. I've spoken out of turn, I'm sorry," she whispered.

I got up from the table to return her contact, and holding her hand I explained that she was the only person that I could rely on. She had my interest at heart, and I assured her that her honesty and experience counted more to me than any internet information, or doctor would advise me.

The next few days went by much like the previous ones; I still had this aversion of going outside, to join the human race, but talking to June each day was my healing.

It was during one of our daily conversations that the idea came to me from June. She was talking about the school her children attended, and how overworked the teachers were.

"Now I am not saying these teachers are bad. They need a medal for just turning up each day, and trying to cope with so many kids in one room. I know in some of them fancy private schools they have teacher aides or volunteers. That's not the case in St John's. I don't think they have the budget to cover assistants. Volunteers; well, that's a hopeless case, who would volunteer? Mothers, like me, either work or have too many young ones that take their time and energy. Them who have the time wouldn't want to spend it in that 'Glory Hole' looking after other people's kids."

She continued polishing and vacuuming, which cut short this conversation for that day. As I was tired I chose to retreat to my bedroom to nap.

I lay on the bed listening to the hum of the vacuum, not able to sleep and pondering the situation at St John's school. My thoughts wandered into the areas I could help. I loved books; maybe I could read to the children or help them to read. Then I dismissed this thought. I had no experience with children, no teaching qualifications, and what on earth would George say if he knew I was spending my time in that area of town? The vacuum stopped, and I steadily dozed.

That evening I tried to talk to George about getting out of the house and doing something rewarding. It was a hopeless task. 'Something rewarding' for George meant earning money.

"There is no necessity for you to go back to work, my business is coming together quicker than I thought. I will need you by my side soon. We have some invitations in the pipeline that are important for you and me to attend. I hope you will be up to it, and ready to go when I know the dates."

"Will these events take place in the evening or at the weekend?" I questioned.

"Now I don't have precise details yet, my secretary deals with that. What a curious question, Dear."

He then went off at a tangent telling me he had found a gem of a secretary who managed the growing staff, and his new partner with great finesse. His account of this woman surged my envious streak. This in a way shocked me; I had never felt inferior to any woman before. It was evidently clear, just then, that I had to get my self-assurance back, and quickly.

We were eating at the kitchen table a simple casserole that June had prepared when my husband, once more, indicated the way he wanted us to live.

"We must start to have dinner parties again; I have new clients I want to entertain. I think you should go on one of those cookery courses for 'fine dining' and go on line to get some ideas for different table settings and such. Order what you like and then give my secretary the account to pay."

Irritable as I was with his suggestions, I tried to be lighthearted with my answer.

"You really want me to cook for your potential clients? My food would scare them away from you. I think if you want to be safe, we should get a catering company to do this for us."

I finally saw a sweet smile appear on his face, and from across the table he winked at me.

"I am delighted to see you getting back to your old self," he said, still smiling. "The Mary Daniels I married is alive and kicking."

I heard my name being said aloud. Remarkably this small retort resounded in my head. I was a person, who had distinctiveness, my individualism was back.

I was feeling better, I was feeling more confident and after a wonderful night of lovemaking I was finally ready to face the world again.

# Chapter 4
# My Challenge

At first I was hesitant to open my front door, and leave the house. It was like jumping into a swimming pool for the first time. So, I started slowly, I walked out with June, after she had finished her work for the day to her car in the driveway. She understood perfectly the tough undertaking this was for me, and encouraged me in her usually cheerful way. She opened the front door, and gestured with her arm outstretched, jokingly announcing me.

"Ladies and Gentlemen I give you Mrs. Daniels."

Then, holding my elbow she added quietly,

"One step at a time Mrs. Daniels, as the saying goes. You are making a grand entrance to the world that eagerly waits for you."

Her humor made me laugh. In fact I was giggling as I pushed her away, forgetting my fears. I watched her leave the driveway then I looked up to the beautiful sky, and thanked whoever was watching over me for bringing me back to reality, as well as the land of the living. I really had been in a depression, and June had helped me through. Now it was my turn to help her.

For the next few days I went out walking. Thinking with each step how I could make my life more meaningful. The good fresh air brought my appetite back, and the gaunt look of my face disappeared. Physically and mentally I was now ready for a challenge.
I asked George if I could change my car, deceptively telling him that the Mercedes was too big for me to handle, and a smaller car would be more suitable. His answer was pitiful,

"I'll get you a driver, dear, one who will be on tap as you need."

"George, will you listen to what I want for a change." I arrogantly replied.

He was obviously shocked by my retort, and told me so, but his materialistic mentality was not making me content. I wanted another kind of achievement. One that gave me pleasure, however that was not the time for argument so I said I needed to get about again, myself. I wanted to get my confidence back.

This made more sense to him, and he agreed to get me a smaller car, but leave the Mercedes in the garage until I was ready to use it again. That was now acceptable to him.

"One last request George," I added. "Will you let me choose the car? If it is only going to be a temporary arrangement I could buy a second hand car."

"I will let you choose the car, dear, but you certainly are not purchasing a used car. That I am insisting on."

He was paying, he was dictating, therefore, I had to go with his demands, but I had achieved a certain success in my plans.

I looked online to find a car that would not look ostentatious. I wanted a car that would blend into the surroundings. There were many in that category, and once I found just the right one, in black, I called the dealership to let me have a test drive.

The process of choosing the car turned out to be a simple course of action. After I had finished the paper work I referred the salesman to my husband, giving him his office line to complete the purchase.

I was happier than my husband at the choice I made. My Ford Fusion was all I needed to get around. He pouted, and told me as long as it was an interim arrangement he could live with it. Yes, my husband was definitely turning into a snob.

I had contemplated intensely about being a volunteer. I looked at several options, but kept coming back to the same conclusion. Many of the groups needed me at the weekend or in the evening. That would not work out for me. If St John's would let me volunteer, then at least I would have some person in the institute. June was a parent at the school, and knew the right people to contact.

When I told her about my idea I was taken aback when she did not answer me immediately. I thought she would throw her arms around me, and positively confirm to me, that it was a great suggestion. That did not happen. I was finishing my morning coffee, and June was busy emptying the dishwasher, so I thought that maybe she hadn't heard me.

"June, What do you think? Is it something I could manage? Is it a possibility?"

She sat down at the table, and faced me, sympathetically looking directly at me she responded,

"Do you really mean to volunteer at my kids' school? I don't think you truly understand what kind of place it is. Have you ever been to Lower Bridgewater? Where I live is the complete opposite to here. Since the Factory closed down many folks are unemployed, and let me tell you, when you don't have money, then all sorts of bad things happen. The children pick up from their parents, what is right, and what is wrong, and some are not getting the right message. It's not easy for me to keep my kids on the straight and narrow; the older ones listen to their friends and jeer at my opinions. Sometimes, I have to resort to a clip around the ear rather than a pep-talk."

I listened intently as she gave me several illustrations of conflicts, which ended with one or more young person going to prison. Drugs or alcohol were often to blame, and in some families, these vices were available to their children who knew no better.

"This place is not for you, believe me." She concluded, getting up from the table to carry on with her work.

At that point I had nothing to say. My wonderful idea to help others had been shot down in an instance. Furthermore, I knew, in my heart that June's intention was to be candid and honest with me, and maybe I had not thought this plan through.

Then I remembered a statement my Father would declare about socialism.

"If you are not a communist by the time you are 18, then you have no heart, but if you are still a communist when you are 21, then you have no head."

Now I am twice that age, but my head and my heart are in unison. I have a lot to offer, both in brains and money, why should I not share them with the less fortunate?

None of this rhetoric was said out loud. I was still validating my capabilities, I was not completely sure it was realistic or practical for me. Preparation and planning had always been my mantra. Doing what I did know was going to be my first step. Research the project, deal with the unknowns, and then go unafraid into the proposal.

I dropped the subject with June, for the time being. Silently I put my mind-set with the challenge in sight. I was energized. Mary Daniels was alive and kicking again, at last.

Even my husband was noticing the difference in me. I didn't share with him the reason behind my transformation, but lamely told him I was researching the possibility of voluntary work in the community.

"That is an excellent idea, Mary. It's just what a wife of a philanthropist like me should be doing. It can help me immensely. You will meet many like-minded wives of husbands who could be potential clients. My partner's wife does charity volunteering in political circles, hospitals and churches. She spreads her capabilities around for the maximum effect."

As he carried on talking about the wife of his partner, I had to smile. If he only knew where my capabilities were heading, he would have a fit. He definitely would not approve, and absolutely, he would not fund it. The husbands in Lower Bridgewater had no money to invest in my husband's stocks and shares certificates.

I began my mission the next day, informing June and my husband that I was going for a drive in my new car to see how it feels. I headed for Lower Bridgewater.

Driving around the neighborhood I saw a locality just as June had described. The place looked neglected, uncared for and sad. Some of the buildings showed signs of past grandeur. Solid stone structures, two stories high, that were all desperate for repair or a good power wash. Small corner shops seemed to be busy, if the line of push chairs that were outside was anything to go by.

Young men stood around on almost every street corner talking and smoking. As I stopped at the traffic light I watched as the youths whistled and shouted profanities to a young girl who was pushing a baby carriage across the road in front of me.

My heart went out to her, but my head told me she had something I had not got, a baby. The light changed and I decided to go back home before my morbid demeanor returned. I would re-visit Lower Bridgewater when I had more information on the whereabouts of the school, and the pupils who went there.

I came home to a cheerful June, who asked me how I liked my new car.

"I really like it." I told her, "in fact I think I prefer driving it to the Mercedes."

"You are a funny person, Mary; most folks would jump at the chance of driving your beautiful, big reliable car."

I smiled back; nevertheless, not wanting to continue the conversation, I told her I was going to look online to see if there were any reviews relating to Ford Fusion cars. I was not ready to ask June about St John's just yet. I wanted just the facts, not opinions about this subject.

The website about St John's was very informative and surprisingly well done. The picture, which dominated the first page, was of a large stone building built in 1950's, built to last. The façade was imposing; solid stone steps led up to a commanding entrance.

I noted the address, phone numbers and the name of the principal. Then I continued reading. It was now an Elementary school, teaching pupils from Kindergarten to Fifth Grade. The website stated that a decade ago the school's population was over 500 but the numbers were dwindling each year, as more families were leaving the area. It didn't state how many were presently attending. The page seemed to market the school in a very positive way, showing sports, happy children playing in the schoolyard, and pupils working in a library. I closed the page thinking there must be some people around who genuinely cared for St John's. The website seemed to beg for recognition and appreciation.

My next task was to get the directions to the school, and print them out. I intended go the next day to drive by the school. I thought it would be a good idea to get there when the students were arriving for the day, to see for myself what they looked like. I had no sense of what an Elementary pupil was like. My experience with children was truly limited, and that ultimately could possibly go against me. I just had to be prepared for that obstacle, if it surfaced.

I headed for the school the very next day, cautiously excited about my new found project. I needn't have gone to so much trouble printing out the direction as my new little car I found, had a G.P.S. system. It proved to be easy to use, and guided me there without difficulty. I think George must have made sure it had all the bells and whistles before he paid for it.

I recognized the school from the website as soon as I drove by. I decided to park in a safe place near enough for me to observe the Mothers and their children. The multitude of children began slowly, just a few of them being dropped off early by an old car or truck. These were driven by the Fathers, or so it looked to me.
Then more and more of them arrived. Like an army of pushchairs, baby carriages and strollers

they arrived at the school, many of them tugging along the little ones who didn't want to be there.

The older children looked like miniature adults in the way they were dressed, and the younger ones all seemed to be wearing hand-me-downs, that were too small or too big. The scene made me take in a deep breath. The poverty in this area was revealed by the children. The Mothers reflected their anguish in their faces. However, they seemed to have a great sense of comradeship with each other. Groups of them stood around in clusters leaning on the stroller or gripping the toddler's hand as their older children went into the school in groups. Each splinter group of Mothers seemed to know each other well.

They talked and laughed out loud in a social gathering they obviously benefited from, as they were very reluctant to break up. I smiled at the scene and knew in my heart that those women were survivors. The toddlers were playing together using the stones on the ground, or the covers from the push chairs as toys. Ironically, the Mothers seemed to sense when it was time to leave their friends, and before the toddlers became bored with their games, they left their grouping.

I didn't get a sense that these Mothers resented their situations, but that they made the best of it, and got on with their lives. I commended their strength and resilience; furthermore, I knew I needed to learn from them. This thought made me more determined to reach my goal and offer my services.

# Chapter 5
# A Reluctant Socialite

George arrived home late most evenings. We very rarely ate dinner together; consequently I was usually on my computer absorbed in my project when he came in. His usual greeting was shouted from the kitchen,

"I'm home Mary, don't bother to come through I will microwave my plate, and see you later when I've finished."

However, on that evening he added,

"I'll open a bottle of wine later; I have something I would like to discuss with you, if you are not too busy?"

I carefully backed-up my information I had been working on and stored it on my flash drive, and then I erased it from my hard drive. That computer was only used by me; consequently, I had no need to be so fearful of it being seen, but it made me feel better doing it that way. I suppose I wasn't completely confident at that time, and didn't want my 'balloon to be burst' before I had even started on my new vocation.

I went through to the sitting room where George sat pouring wine from the bottle he had uncorked.

"I opened red, I trust that's fine with you?" he said, giving me my glass.

I sat down on the sofa, and placed my glass in front of me on the coffee table. I watched him go through the ritual of sniffing the wine, twirling it around then finally sipping the wine. He obviously was pleased with his choice, as he lifted up his glass in the air, motioning me to raise my glass in the air.

"Cheers, my love, here's to our future, a very fruitful one, so I predict."

I lifted my glass, nodded my head in response, and sipped the wine. I silently told myself to smile and respond positively to what George had to say, however, my racing thoughts were reflecting my own special wishes for the future.

I put down my glass, cocked my head to one side, looking sheepishly towards him. This was the action he was waiting for, and he took only seconds to begin his own egotistic tirade about his business success so far. I continued to nod my head and smile, which encouraged him to continue.

"I want to introduce you to my very important colleagues, my partner, his wife and my excellent secretary. It would be fitting, at this time to invite them to dinner. This, I feel is the essence of good business, and also your part in my venture is about to begin."

He took another sip of wine, waiting for a comment from me. I was lost for words. I didn't want to meet these people, but I wanted to be discreet, however I couldn't come across with the words that would be tactful at that time. I stumbled out a lame excuse instead.

"I don't think I am ready for an occasion like that just now. I want to support you George, but socializing with people… I don't know… scares me. I need more time to get back to normal. I would be awful company and no asset at all for you."

He poured more wine for himself then, sighed. He evidently didn't buy my excuse because he continued to provide me with details of how he intended the evening to be arranged.

"You will have nothing to do at all, dear. Maybe go to the beauty parlor, buy yourself a new cocktail dress, and just leave the rest to me and my secretary."

I was beginning to hate this secretary woman before I even saw her. What did he need me for? Was I a trophy for him to show off to his friends? Had our marriage come to this?

"I would not know what to talk about George. I have no idea of what goes on in the financial world of today, especially your world."

"Then just sit genially, and let me do the talking, dear, that can't be too hard to do?"

Now that statement rang true. George no longer listened to me or concerned himself with my opinions. We had gone astray from the jovial discussions we used to have.

He finished the bottle himself, and I politely sat there listening as he told me about a reputable catering company he would employ. They would set up the whole evening plus clearing it all away. The conversation was over as far as George was concerned. I emptied my glass, and told him I was going to bed as the wine had made me sleepy. Yet another untruth from me; they were beginning to escalate and that fact scared me.

I awoke next morning, alone in bed, which was surprising, but not deterring. I looked at the clock and it was 8.30a.m. I didn't know if George had slept beside me, and left for work, or if he slept downstairs because of all the good wine he drank. Either way I was not eager to talk about the upcoming event that George was determined to arrange, whether I liked it or not.

My motivation to get out of bed was to carry on with my own plans. I showered, washed my hair, and then, I joined June in the kitchen.

"You've just missed Mr. Daniels; he passed me on my way in. The coffee is still hot, would you like me to make you some toast?"

I had an ulterior motive in accepting June's offer as I wanted more information from her. I opened the conversation gently regarding St John's, and carefully expanded on the truth, which was regretfully becoming a tendency with me recently.

I had researched the Principal's name and background, and found out she had graduated from my Alma Mater. I told June there was a function coming up at the University that I considered the Principal might want to attend.

"I thought I would ask her in person instead of on the telephone, or through the school secretary. Do you think I should call the secretary first to make an appointment; is she an amiable person?"

"Miss Snooty Pants, amiable, no way, the title of secretary has gone to her head. You can't get to Miss Jenkins in the Principal's office without passing through her office and giving her title and verse about your reason for wanting to see the Principal. Every time I've tried it, I've gotten nowhere near. She's told me all sorts of reasons why. Like, 'the Principal is not in today,' or 'she's too busy,' or 'would I like to make an appointment?' I've resorted in talking to the teachers to try to sort out my concerns."

I took the toast, and let her continue at length; to describe the various troubles she had to sort out with the teachers of her 5 children. I answered sympathetically as each incident was explained, hoping she would finally give me the information I wanted to hear.

"Then what do you think would be the best way for me?" I asked coaxingly.

"Oh! You'd have no problem getting an appointment. Your accent and manner would get you through the door."

We both laughed out loud as she mimicked my accent. I was pleased I had June on board to enter her vicinity, with the right approach. I went to the study to immediately call the secretary.

I took June's advice and, in fact, put on more of the 'posh' accent than I normally used. I told the secretary very little about the reason for my visit to the Principal,. Nevertheless, I stressed that we had both attended the same University, and hadn't seen each other for ages.

This seemed to impress her profusely and her response to me, I detected, was one of obliging pleasure that a University friend of her boss was coming to visit, and she would make sure the Principal would be free tomorrow afternoon around 2.00.

So, my plan was at last in motion. I spent the next few hours thinking of how I would approach the Principal with my offer to be a volunteer. Obviously, my fake voice would only be used with the school secretary, and my fortunate discovery that the Principal and I had the same Alma Mater was a definite starting point of my proposal. I knew I was over thinking this situation, so I decided to go back to the kitchen and chit-chat with my cheerful, down to earth help.

I told her about the conversation with the school secretary. I purposely dramatized the dialogue, using my fake voice, with the school secretary's charmed response. She began to laugh so much that she had to sit down at the kitchen table to recover.

"What did I tell you? She's out of her depth with people who don't live in our area. She can't boss you around, since you went to the same University as her boss."

She spoke the last few words in a dignified voice before rolling her eyes, and chuckling at her own accent. June's laugh was infectious and we both enjoyed the fool around so much that the paper napkins on the kitchen table had to be used to wipe our eyes.

Finally, I got up from the table, suggesting I was keeping June from finishing her chores. I thanked her for the happy interlude, which I meant sincerely, but excused myself by saying I had to go to find an appropriate outfit to wear.

"Don't forget the tiara," she laughingly called as I left the kitchen.

# Chapter 6
# My first steps to a new life

Next morning I made sure I was up early enough to make George his breakfast so I could sit with my coffee, and tell him my half-truth about how I was going to spend my day. I had to cover myself in case June had related to him some of our chat.

I waited until he was enjoyably tucking in to his large omelet then I said,

"I'm meeting a friend from my Alma Mater this afternoon. I have just found out that she lives around here."

"That's nice Mary; I am pleased you are beginning to get out and about with your friends again. There is plenty in our account, in case you go shopping, or if you take her to lunch."

"Thank you, George, but I think we will only be going for coffee as she has to get back to work."

He raised his eyebrows, quickly finished the rest of the omelet, drained his coffee cup, and then stood facing me.

"Maybe you should ask your friend to join us for our upcoming dinner night. The more the merrier, I think is the saying. Oh, I forgot to tell you we have arranged it for next Saturday. Don't forget to buy a new cocktail dress before then."

He headed for the front door, then put on his jacket, picked up his briefcase and left me pondering on his last words. "We have arranged" I suppose that inferred his secretary and he had arranged, without even considering if next Saturday would be convenient for me. I was livid. I even thought of calling his secretary to say that I had a previous engagement for that night and couldn't attend, except that would not work. George knew I never went out at night.

To simmer down, I decided to have a leisurely bath before I went on my planned appointment. My anger was beginning to turn into sorrow and self-pity, and that was not a mood I wanted to be in before I met Miss Jenkins.

I lay in the bath reflecting on the change in my husband's demeanor. We seemed to be drifting apart since we lost the baby. We scarcely had the banter conversations that I always enjoyed, our discussions had become one sided. I felt my husband had a condescending attitude towards me.

"For heavens' sake I lost a baby not my mind." I said out loud.

At that moment I recognized I had to change. I had to be active again and use my capabilities. Dwelling on the past was eating away at my intrinsic worth. I needed to leap out of my comfort zone, to open up the options myself. The Mary Daniels of old had been misplaced not lost. From that day on, I vowed to myself to make changes in my life, and accept the consequences.

I smiled at the inspirational pep talk I had just given myself. I rubbed my skin with the sponge, invigorating, refreshing, revitalizing my body to get ready for the task ahead. My mind and body were all set for the challenge.

I wrapped a large soft bath towel around myself, and went into the closet to choose my outfit. I selected a light brown pantsuit that had always been a good standby in the past when I met clients for the first time. It was smart yet casual, and fitted the situation appropriately.

It was still too early to leave for St John's so I decided to eat some lunch – no need for me to eat out. I would pamper myself with a pot of Earl Grey tea. My mood had changed, I was enjoying the transformation. It's wonderful what a nice long bath and a good pot of tea can amend.

Just after one o clock I was ready to leave. I didn't want to be too early or too late so I drove steadily through Lower Bridgewater to get the feel of the surroundings. I did a number of detours before parking in the school car park, and then I went up the stone steps, through its imposing front entrance, into the school.

There was a young pupil in the entrance hall so I asked the way to the secretary's office, which turned out to be the first door in this hallway. The keeper of the fortress was guarding her globe of authority at the front access.

I opened the door. This reception room had three wooden chairs against the back wall with a small window on the facing wall that had a notice that said 'ring for attention'. I pressed the button and the window was slid open. A stern looking lady appeared and asked what I wanted. After explaining who I was, she apologized in that phony tone of voice, and asked me to go through into her office.

"Miss Jenkins will be with you shortly; she is just taking a telephone call. Please take a seat."

The chairs in this office were a little more comfortable than the ones in the reception, but she, nevertheless apologized for them. I was about to take a seat when the door opened, and a rather rotund woman asked me to come through to her office, and then she told me to sit. This was a comfortable padded armchair.

She smiled and sat opposite me behind her desk. Although she was small, her large desk and chair was an appropriate height, and width for the room.

This lady I liked straight away.

"Mrs. Daniels, I believe?"

"Yes I am. Thank you for fitting me into your busy schedule." I began; however, with a curious look she interrupted me before I could go on.

"Excuse me, but you look familiar to me. Was your name Mary Price before you married?"

Startled with the fact she knew my name before I married, I slowly responded.

"Yes I was."

Then the most unusual exchange took place. All my planning and research could not have prepared me for this.

"Well! Mary Price you were my idol. You were a year ahead of me, and I wanted to be like you. I joined the Drama Society and the Debating Team just to see you and hear your voice. I looked up to you and tried to mimic your expressions and your deportment. Of course, I was too heavy and clumsy to pull it off, but I practiced hard to get the pronunciations correct. Your self- confidence and manner were qualities I pined for."

I looked at this happy, successful woman and could not believe what she was telling me. I shook my head in disbelief and smiled.

She spoke on the intercom to her secretary and asked for some coffee and biscuits, adding that she would not be available the rest of the afternoon unless it was an emergency.

"You see, food was always my downfall, and I still find it irresistible. You will stay a little while so we can catch up on old times?"

Over coffee and biscuits we chatted easily together about situations we both remembered, as well as people that we liked or disliked. We talked openly about our years after college. She told me that her ambition had always been to come back to Lower Bridgewater, and help the less fortunate.

"At least I was successful in that goal," she said with a giggle.

I conveyed to her about my marriage to George, and losing the baby and my self-esteem. She was sympathetic but not morbid, and changed the subject abruptly.
"What on earth brought you here, surely not to see me? Oh! By the way, please call me Barbara, and do you mind if I call you Mary?"

I could never have imagined my plan going so smoothly, but I was cautious not to push the issue forward too soon. I asked her about the positives and negatives in her job, bypassing, for a time, the reason for my visit.

She was anxious to share with me her love for her profession, and for the children she worked with. She told me her aspirations for them were high, but that their social and economic backgrounds held them back. She waxed at length about individual pupils who had great potential, and could have attended college, but their families needed them to find a job, or babysit the younger children while the Mother went out to work.

I broached the subject cautiously. "What are the things you need to make your life here at the school better? Do you have enough resources?"

"Well, it depends on what you call resources. Textbooks I have, the county is very good at providing in that area, because they are keen to keep the Standard Assessment test in check. However, this is a poor area of the county, and our challenges are much greater than the other richer neighborhoods. Our parents don't have the time, or ability to help their children with homework or reading."

"Would it help if you had more staff? I asked cautiously.

"Of course, but I don't have the budget for that."

I sensed an opening, which I leapt into. "Do you think it would be possible for me to come in to help the teachers some days? I can find a little time here and there to help out. I wouldn't need to be reimbursed, I don't know the logistics of having volunteers in your classrooms, but I am sure you could find out."

I didn't expand on this point, because I had already researched this area, and found out it was at the discretion of the governing body. Nevertheless, I wanted Barbara to find out, for herself.

"I can't believe you would do this for me, I mean for us. It would be a tremendous help, and good resource for my teachers, they are so overburdened with the necessary official paperwork, trying to keep order, as well as teach. They would be fighting over the possibility of support in their classrooms. Leave it with me and I will find out and let you know. I can personally vouch for your capabilities," she said with a smile.

I stood up and told her how much I had enjoyed our meeting. I offered my hand across the desk saying, "I must let you get on with your work. Just call me, if you have any outcome to my offer." Silently I was hoping to get out before the obvious question was going to be asked, but I didn't succeed

She grasped my hand with both her hands and asked, "you never did get round to saying why you came to St John's today."

I fumbled to find an answer, but eventually I resorted to yet another deception. I told her that the University had contacted me to try to recruit more Alma Maters to the next anniversary reception. They had had a very poor response to their invitation, and were hoping I could help. I added, with baited breath, that her name was on the local list they had sent me.

Still holding my hands she answered that she wasn't comfortable going to social events, furthermore she hadn't the time to go out of State at that point of time.

We finally walked to the door together, still holding hands, and after a polite embrace, and a kiss on the cheek, she walked out in front of me to her secretary's office, where she addressed her secretary in a very business-like manner.
"I hope I will be seeing my good friend very soon. Remember her name, and keep note of her telephone number." Then she turned to me, and with a formal farewell we parted company.

I walked to my car in a bemused way. The outcome of that meeting was totally unpredictable. I was elated yet cautiously apprehensive of the result. My hopes and expectations for my future were definitely going forward. I knew my new venture was not conclusive; nevertheless a big step forward had been made that day.

# Chapter 7
# My Other Life

I was surprised when I looked at the clock in the car how late it was. I had enjoyed the afternoon so much. The house was empty, no one was in, and everything was tidy and clean. I went through to the kitchen, and saw a note on the table. June had been busy, but she had prepared a casserole for us, knowing I had an appointment at St John's; it was in the oven ready to be heated. There was a big smiley face drawn at the bottom of the page with the salutation – 'hope you enjoyed my neck of the woods!'

I was feeling in great spirits when my husband called to say he would not be late, and if I wanted, we could go out to dinner. I made the lame excuse that I had been out for lunch with my friend, so didn't want to go out again. I added that June had made a casserole for us, which would be ready when he got home. He accepted my refusal, but added that the casserole would keep.

"George, thank you but, no thank you. See you soon." I retorted determinedly.

"O.K. Mary, just thought it would be nice for us to go out, and be seen. I'll be home in an hour."

I put down the receiver reflecting on his remark. Why would we want to be seen? Who would care if we were dining out or not? We could have a pleasant conversation together at home, rather than in a noisy restaurant. I think Barbara and I had that in common. We both preferred a small social gathering, rather than large one.

True to form, George arrived home within the hour, carrying a bouquet of flowers.

"There you are, dear," he said, handing me the flowers.

"What are these for?' I asked

"Nothing special, Mary, just for being you, I trust you like the selection that Glenda, my secretary, chose?"

"Thank you, George." I answered, silently thinking he couldn't even choose a bunch of flowers himself. Still the thought was there, I hoped. As I was putting the flowers into the vase he came behind me, and kissed my neck.

"Let's open a bottle of wine; I have plenty to tell you tonight."

"Fine by me, you go to choose," sarcastically thinking maybe he could do that for himself these days without his secretary, I also became aware he was on first name terms with his new secretary.

Dinner that night began awkwardly, at least for me. He asked a lot of questions about the meeting with my friend that day, and the more information he inquired about, the more I stretched the truth. I knew I couldn't share with him the true reason for my visit to St John's nor the plans I had for volunteering there. George's plan for me, which I was shortly going to find out, was totally different.

"Well, my Dear I want you to raise your glass and join me in a toast to my new company. Daniels, Portman and Turner, L.L.C." He said this in a self-important way that made me cringe, but nevertheless, I did as I was told, and raised my glass.

"I did know you had a partner called Portman, who, you told me was a Corporate Lawyer, so who is Turner?" I asked just to sound interested.

He was eager to explain that Mr. James Turner was another lawyer with a great deal of wealthy contacts, who were looking for investments.

"Brad, that is Brad Portman, persuaded him to join us, and I have to say this guy really does know the markets. He thinks we should open another office soon."

"Is that not a little impetuous," I suggested, "you have only just started the new company?"

He brushed off my remark by offering me more wine, and never responded to my suggestion. In fact he went on at length to explain to me about growing portfolios, certificates of deposits, and having the right secretary to keep the records. All his colleagues were praised in order of priority. However, my mind was elsewhere, thinking about my successful day. I wasn't really listening and didn't realize he had changed the subject back to the proposal of a dinner party at our home.

"So what do you think, Mary are you happier with that option?"

Because I hadn't followed his digression, I was reluctant to answer, so asked him to explain the option in more detail.

"Mrs. Turner, James's wife, has invited us to dine at their home, just the six of us. She thinks it would be appropriate for us all to get to know each other and celebrate."

"I would not fit in George, I'm not corporate minded, I wouldn't know what to say or answer. I don't want to be a burden for you."

"There you go again, undermining yourself. You are a very intelligent woman, and a very beautiful one at that, so let me show you off, let them see my wife has beauty as well as brains." He said with enthusiasm. "There will be no declining from this invitation from us, it is too important. I want to see you on Saturday, ready to leave at seven in all your finery. Please, Mary, don't spoil it all for me. Go with your new friend to shop, and she will help you choose the clothes that suit your wonderful figure."

"Alright, George, I will do this for you. I'll try not to embarrass you with my clothes, or my talk."

He got up from his chair to squeeze my shoulders, followed by a kiss on the cheek. "You could never do that. Mary, you are my wife."

I didn't understand whether his last remark was a compliment to me or to him, but I allowed it to pass.

I couldn't imagine asking Barbara to go with me to shop for clothes, I'm sure it would not be her favorite thing to do, nor really was it mine. The following morning I decided to go to my closet, to see what was in there, I was sure I had some cocktail dresses, and accessories pushed at the back that would save me the trouble of shopping.

Sure enough there was. It had been such a long time since I had worn this kind of style I wondered if it would still fit, or if it was out of fashion. I laid several dresses out on top of the bed, then I put back some of the more glitzy ones. There was a light grey one that I always felt comfortable wearing, this I kept as a possibility. A midnight blue dress and a black one were also promising choices. Now to the test to see if they still fitted.

I pinned my hair up and began to try on. In reality they all were too loose, I must have lost weight or changed shape since the baby. I knew that most people after having a baby put on weight, maybe my state of mind had resulted in the opposite happening. I decided to try on some high heels to see if that made me look different. As I was staring in to the mirror I heard June singing as she was vacuuming in the hallway outside my bedroom. I opened the door, and tried to get her attention.

"My, you startled me," she said as she switched off the vacuum. "It's a bit early to go out on the town isn't it?" She remarked seeing me in an evening dress.

I explained about the business dinner party that I grudgingly had to attend, which was the reason I was trying on dresses. I asked her to come into the bedroom, and help me choose. I trusted June's opinion even though my dresses were not something she was familiar with; she knew me and therefore, would say which suited me best.

Together we opted for the black one, which was 'classy' so June thought, and I knew in the past it had been a good standby for many occasions. I looked in the long mirror and June came up behind me and put her two hands on my waist to gather up the loose material.

"This could be an easy fix, would you like me to do it?"

"Can you do such an alteration?" I asked with surprise.
"With as many kids as I have and very little to spend on new clothes I have no other option, but to make the hand me downs fit. I know this will be a doddle of a job. I'll have it finished and out of the dry cleaners well before next Saturday, no problem. That's if you are happy with me doing just that."

I hugged her tightly, and told her I would love her to do it, moreover I would pay her for her work and the dry cleaning. I had an emergency sewing box in my bedside table that I rarely used, where I found some straight pins for June to use to get the fit right. I smiled at my reflection, and was satisfied.

"I will put it in a bag before you leave. Oh! June please keep this arrangement discrete, between us. Mr. Daniels wants me to spend a fortune on impressing his partners, and I honestly don't think they will notice if my outfit is new or not. My husband certainly won't expect it not to be new."

She left the room to carry on working. While I still had the dress on I went to my dressing table to look in my jewelry box, and found what I was looking for, a simple string of pearls with matching earrings. Not real, but very good imitations. The task was done in a way I was content with. Now I only had to keep my composure and poise inside to look good outside. Actually this made me feel more single minded to carry out this ruse in the materialistic world my husband had joined.

I read once that Coco Chanel would wear a mixture of fake and real jewelry to amuse herself, because she was so rich and famous everybody assumed that all her jewelry was genuine. With that thought in mind I began to look forward to the dinner. I had a challenge to look forward to. I sensed I was becoming more conniving, but then I was also developing my self-confidence. I was actually daring myself to enjoy the portentous dinner party.

# Chapter 8
# The Call

The call came from Barbara, but unfortunately, I was out at the library. However, she had left a message for me to call her back. The message didn't indicate whether it was good or bad news, so I nervously returned the call.

Of course, it was answered by her secretary, who recognized my voice and my number, however, with a supercilious, reluctant apology she told me that Miss Jenkins was not able to take the call at that time, and would it be possible for me to call back in about one hour.

I didn't want to sound too eager, so I obliged, and ended the short conversation. My stomach was churning, so I went into the kitchen to eat some lunch. I thought about my weight loss, which I honestly had not taken notice of, and decided to make myself a large plate of scrambled eggs on toast, adding cheese and tomato to the mix.

Without a doubt I had over faced myself with the portion, but I decided to take it slowly, and read the newspaper. This made it easier for me to overcome my un-enthusiasm for food. Little by little I finished the plate, and felt well again. I resolved to take better care of myself in the future in order for me to be ready for whatever came my way. At that moment the telephone rang.

It was Barbara, who apologized for not being there when I called; she told me it was because she had been called to deflate a classroom fight.

"All in a day's work," she meekly explained.

Then she started to tell me in detail about her correspondence, and further phone calls with the Governors of St John's. Her precise, detailed account was exasperating, but perhaps it was a professional trait after years of teaching. I didn't interrupt in case she went off at a tangent from the news I wanted to hear. Finally she came to the point,

"They have agreed to let you come into the school on a voluntary basis, however you have to sign some kind of liability insurance, which I will look over for you, and check if is reasonable, that is if you are still willing to help us at St John's?"

Again, I didn't want to sound too keen; on the other hand, I did need Barbara to realize I was sincere in my offer, but she made the progress of my aim uncomplicated.

"Maybe, if you came in one day a week to begin with? Just to see if you can deal with the situation? I promise I won't start you off with the rebels until you feel you can handle the nonconformist element of the school," she said with humor in her voice.

This suited me perfectly. It would give me time to adjust to the challenge and to discover if I was up to the test. It would ease me into the work, and also help me to find out just where I could be the most functional.

"Of course I can do that, just let me know what day of the week, and what time, and I will sort out my calendar around it." I said hoping she wouldn't guess it was the only thing I truly wanted to do more than anything else.

"Could you start next week? How about next Monday, the start of the week? You could observe different grade levels, and get to know the school, our pupils and staff. Then you will be able to see where you think you would best fit in, afterwards we could discuss it."

Barbara sounded very logical, but excited as she quickly told me her offer. She was raring to go, and so was I. I agreed to her proposal and asked what time I should arrive.

"Well, we have school morning assembly at eight fifteen, is that going to be too early for you?"

"No," I answered with a chuckle, "I shall be at your office at eight." Then I added, "I am really looking forward to it Barbara. See you Monday."

I put down the receiver and was surprised to see my hand shaking. In the pit of my stomach the butterflies were fluttering. This was not from hunger this time, but from sheer excitement, apprehension and anticipation to succeed in my mission.

Once my body had calmed down, with the help of a good cup of coffee, I realized that I had a big obstacle to overcome. If I was to be up and ready to go so early on Monday, then I had some explaining to do to George.

My scheming mind was working overtime on this quest. Doing voluntary work in Lower Bridgewater would not be something that George would condone. Nor could I say I was helping out in St John's school classroom, which would really freak him out. I went back on my computer to look again at St John's website really to get more information to help me fit in on Monday. There was a fact that inspired my interest. St John's school was affiliated to St John's church and they regularly needed donations of flowers to adorn their dim interior. There was a contact name to get in touch with, which I took note of, and hoped I could convince George that I was going there to offer flowers, or maybe plants for their cause.

The following evening I brought the subject up for his approval. His response,

"The intention is very good dear, but I don't want you in that area of town at all. I can send them a large donation to buy flowers, in your name of course, if you want me to."

My idea was not going well; I had to pursue it further.

"It's just that I have promised my good friend I would go with her next week. She buys the flowers, and then arranges them for the church. They haven't got anyone to do that, so I promised I would help." Then pushing the trickery further I added, "Her husband knows the clergy there, and he is very big in the community."

"The husband or the clergy is influential?" he asked on impulse.

"Both I think." I responded, knowing I had sparked an interest.

"I am not happy about the location Mary, but I suppose you can handle yourself. When are you going to ask your friend, and her husband to dinner?" he asked.

I was dropping down into a depth of deception I was definitely not happy with. I hated the idea of not being honest and straightforward with my husband, however my instincts told me the alternate confrontation about this matter would be more than I could contend with at that time. I was not strong enough to battle with him about good deeds, helping the needy or giving back to society. George would certainly not agree, unless he could be observed by the right people, to be bestowing gifts to society.

I decided to brush off his remark by asking about the upcoming dinner party. Telling him I had my outfit ready, and I was sure it would be suitable. I told him I was eagerly anticipating the event, which was the truth, but for an erroneous reason.
I listened for the next hour to my self-absorbed husband expand on the values of his new contemporaries, and about the valuable example we could set as a couple to benefit his position in the company. Finally he told me how thankful he was for me to accept this event in the way he knew I eventually would.

I kissed him and told him I had to call my friend, knowing deep down that I had won half the battle by agreeing to go to his precious dinner party. The leverage I had was to find the middle ground, to accept his charades in order to pursue my true aims. The way to accomplish them would have to be, compromise.

# Chapter 9
# The display of Pretention

Saturday came all too soon for me, but nevertheless I was ready to play my expected role as the wife of the ambitious, devoted husband. June had made a fine job of the alteration, and the dry cleaning of the dress gave it the 'new' look I was hoping for. The basic string of pearls along with the simple black shoes with a small heel added to the appearance I aimed for. I felt comfortable, and that was important. I loosely pinned up my hair to fall naturally around my face, which I was happy with for an evening out.

George was waiting for me in the sitting room, already sipping his first cocktail, and actually gasped at me, in a pleasant way, as I came through the door.

"Mary, you look absolutely fantastic. You and your friend choose wisely, I must say she has a very good taste of fashion."

I blushed at the compliment, secretly relieved he was hooked by my fabrication, and the thought of June accepting his flattering remark brought a smile to my face. My next step was to hope that his partners, and their wives, would equally approve of my appearance, but actually, even though George was hoping for that outcome, I was not concerned either way.

"Is it really a good idea to be drinking so early in the evening George?" I asked, concerned about the driving.

"I have ordered a driver for the evening, dear, so we both can relax and enjoy ourselves, it also gives the right impression to our hosts."

This kind of behavior was something new in our lives. Over indulgence had never been something George involved himself with, especially in our early years. He was budget minded to the core, and this change of directions made me feel uncomfortable. However, I justified his actions to myself by accepting that drinking and driving was not acceptable, also I knew, he would not have allowed me to drive that night.

As we waited for the driver I decided to join George, and have a drink, at least it would steady my nerves. The drink loosened his tongue so; yet again I had to hear about his rapid growth in business, and the fortunate merger of the three partners. I looked down to the floor and realized my skirt length, as I sat down, could be a problem, then the doorbell rang, our driver had arrived.

The ride to the Turner's house took about thirty minutes. It was in an extremely affluent part of town. The driver stopped outside the large gate, where he pressed the button for the intercom, to announce our arrival.

Immediately the automatic gates opened to let us through to a long driveway that led to the impressive house. I nervously looked down at my modest black dress, and wondered if I had chosen wisely. All the same, it was too late the massive double front doors were opened, and standing there were our host and hostess, waiting to personally greet us.

George had a big beaming smile on his face as the driver first let me out before going round for him. All this personal attention he was getting pleasure from. I didn't approach the Turners myself, I preferred to wait for George to take my arm, and lead me to their world of opulence.

My husband introduced me, with a flamboyant wave of his hand, and to my surprise, the lady of the house took it from him and kissed both my cheeks, well not really, she brushed the side of her cheek along mine. Then she spoke in a very phony British accent,

"Lovely to see you Mary, how delightful you look." Which I hoped was a compliment. "Welcome to my home, and please call me Caroline." She added.

George was walking in front with her husband James, and we followed them through to their imposing lounge area, which looked to me more like a museum than a home. The chairs looked too delicate to sit on, even for my slender build, also the drapes seemed too heavy and dark.

I presumed the other two people in the room were Mr. and Mrs. Portman, and George took me over to introduce me. They were, indeed Mr. Brad Portman and his wife Vicky.

I was relieved everyone was standing, it was more comfortable for me as I was afraid my dress would show too much leg if I sat down. However, it didn't take long before Vicky complimented me on my appearance.

"How do you keep your figure, darling? I exercise with my trainer three times a week, and still don't have your shape. You must give me the name of your instructor."

I was saved from answering as another person entered the room. A tall, dignified, middle-aged woman dressed in a flowing silk dress. She stopped while her name was announced to the room by Mr. Turner,

"For those who don't know, this is our company's, incalculable, inexhaustible secretary, Ms. Glenda Morris." He announced.

The statuesque woman nodded her head from side to side, and then took the glass offered by Mr. Turner, and walked to unite with her masculine admirers.

The evening had only just begun, but already I was sick of the false salutations, and their forced indifferent remarks. By the end of the evening I was worn out. The men had mostly dominated the conversations, with Ms. Glenda offering her forthright opinion on several topics. However, the wives, it seemed, were there sorely to ornate the table setting, and hopefully support their spouses' remarks.

Mercifully, it was not to be a late evening, and when our car arrived at nine thirty, I was eager to leave this obnoxious company, to get back to my sane, unassuming home. The goodbyes were performed by each couple, in turn brushing each cheek whilst gripping, at a safe distance, the hands. The embraces were rigid, cold, and uneasy. I went home in silence, since George was napping as a result of having too many cognacs. The car stopped at our house, and thankfully, George awoke in time to pay the driver. I got out, hastily telling him I was rushing in to go to the bathroom.

It was my retreat, my place of solitude, to shut out the memories of a pretentious world.

# Chapter 10
# Finding My Niche

Driving to St John's that Monday morning was both exhilarating and fearful for me. I decided to put the radio on, and listen to music to calm my nerves. Perhaps it was because I had been a long time out of the work place or maybe I was uneasy about my ability to fit into this alien environment. I knew I had to change my mindset before I reached the school, if I was to be a useful asset to Barbara. As a result, I thought about the alternative, looking back at the women at the dinner party, wondering how they were starting their Monday morning, which changed my mood. I was ready to face my choice.

I made my way to Barbara's office without being delayed by the secretary. She had obviously been told of my arrival, and ushered me through the door with a hospitable greeting. Barbara stood up from her desk, and with a beaming smile said,

"I'm so very glad you didn't change your mind, welcome to St John's. I have told the staff about you volunteering, and they are all eager to claim your help. In a few minutes we will go to the large hall for morning assembly, would you like some coffee or water before we go? Please, Mary sit down, and I will explain what I have planned for your first day."

My mouth was very dry, at that point, but before I could reply, in walked the secretary with a tray of both coffee and water on it. I eagerly drank a sip of water, and then while Barbara told me her intentions for me, I finished the coffee as well.

She asked if I could spare the time to be there a full day or just for the morning, and I replied that I wanted to see a full day at the school to understand and experience what I may be required to do. This pleased her immensely, and after we both had finished our coffee, we made our way to the hall.

Walking through the corridor I reminisced about my own school days, which were a happy time, and I was in high spirits as I followed Barbara up the steps and on to the platform. There was a line of chairs, all vacant, but I chose to sit on the last one. Barbara stood behind the podium sorting out her notes.

The children entered in an orderly fashion with each teacher leading their class to the designated area, and then joining me on the stage. The teachers were a mixture of both men and women, of all ages. All of them gave me a welcome smile and a nod before they sat down.

Once the hall was full, Barbara held up her hand, and miraculously the murmuring and whispering stopped.

"Well children," she began, "I expect you are all wondering who the new person is. The lady sitting on the end chair is Mrs. Daniels, and she is here to help you and your teachers. You won't see her every day, but I want you all to show her how good you can be, and then maybe she will come in more often."

The assembly began with the 'Oath of Allegiance' followed by a hymn they all seemed to know; at least most of the words, with the loud support of their teachers   Finally, Barbara gave out her notices. Throughout the whole assembly I had a warm feeling, a happy and contented feeling that I was in the right place. I was prepared to face the day ahead with keen enthusiasm.

By the end of the day I was exhausted, even though I had only been observing. I made copious notes of areas where I guessed I could help, and questions that were relevant to the curriculum. I was amazed and astonished at how the teachers, in most of the classrooms, managed to keep order and teach.

I meant to see Barbara before leaving that day, but she was occupied elsewhere, so I told the school secretary I would call Miss Jenkins that evening.

I returned home to a quiet place. The silence made me feel awkward after the hustle and bustle of the school. I switched on the television to provide me with company while I made myself a pot of tea. I hadn't informed June where I was going that day, so she had not prepared anything for dinner; however I knew I could get something delivered later.

I looked at the television, which was showing the news, and was stunned at the recognizable faces I was seeing. It was some political fund-raising function, and there in the center of the screen was my husband with James Turner. I turned up the sound just in time to hear the interviewer asking James about his support for the political candidate, which she suspected was substantial. He dodged the issue by proclaiming the attributes of Mr. Swift, the candidate, as George was nodding his head, and smiling in agreement by his side.

I was shocked. My husband had never; in all our married life, shown any interest in politics. In fact, at the last election he proclaimed that, all politicians were the same, promising you everything before, but doing nothing positive after they got in. He didn't share with me his intention of going to that luncheon, when I was making hard work of where I was going for the day. I was determined to ask him outright about his public appearance at the fund-raiser.

I rang his cell, and while it was ringing my confidence waned. He answered straight away.

"Hallo, Mary, you are back home I see. Is everything O.K?"

"Yes, no problems, but ..." I stammered, "I haven't had time to sort out what we should have for dinner, shall I order a takeaway?"

"Don't bother about me darling, I have had a large business lunch with the partners. Just order for yourself, I don't know how late I will be. Excuse me Mary, I am being called."

Then the conversation abruptly ended, without giving me time to put forward the real purpose of my call. The news program had moved to a different topic so I switched it off, trying to erase the previous event from my mind.

I went to the kettle to pour the hot water, and realized my hands were shaking; I had to sit down and recover, my mind was racing all over the place. Questions with no answers, then the phone rang. Maybe, I thought, George was calling me to explain, but it was Barbara.

She apologized for not being there when I left, and asked me about my day. I was still mesmerized by the news program, and couldn't get back to the realities of my day. I made a meager excuse about being busy at that time, and asked if I could see her tomorrow at the school to discuss my notes.

"Oh, certainly, I am sorry to disturb your evening. I do forget that married folks have another life besides work. I will look forward to seeing you tomorrow; can you make it around 2.00?"

I told her I would be there, and wished her a good evening. I placed the receiver down, my hands still nervously sweating. I hoped Barbara nor her staff had been watching the news that night, and then I realized, they didn't know my husband. I was really freaking out.

It was late when George arrived home, but he didn't share with me the reason. I noticed he went straight to the liquor cabinet, and poured himself a large whisky. This, again, was not a customary habit of his, but recently it was becoming a regular occurrence.

He took off his necktie and his jacket before sitting down to enjoy his drink. I sat facing him determined to ask this time about the fund-raiser.

"I saw you on television this evening. I didn't know you were into politics. It was quite a shock for me …." I didn't have time to continue, as George quickly interrupted.

"Now, Mary it is something that you just might have to get used to. James says we must be seen and noticed in the best circles. That's what is needed, if we expect to grow our business the way our projected business plans are intended. The three of us have been working overtime to concede on our master plan. It's very exciting, the direction we hope our policies and procedures will take us. You may see your husband more often in the public eye, so I suppose you will have to get used to it."

He made his last statement in a finite way, which asked for no rebuff from me. His predetermined life-style was going to change whether I liked it or not, and silently I thought, so will mine.

# Chapter 11
# Stretching my Horizons

The next morning I lay in bed until I heard George leave for work. I didn't want a lecture, or to play the justification game he wanted me to participate in. I had made up my mind I would follow my work option, and leave George to pursue his choices. I was not happy with the way our marriage was going, we were drifting apart; our values and principals were not the same anymore. George didn't converse with me; he made statements that sounded like orders, which he required me to accept. My husband had changed; he was not the man I had married, but if he was busy in his new life then he wouldn't have time to interfere in mine, and that thought was my redeemer.

June was in the kitchen when I came down, so I decided to share my recent visits to St John's with her. Over breakfast, I told her about the school governors agreeing to my volunteering, and how well I got along with Miss Jenkins. It turned out her children had told her about a 'new teacher' who had come to their school yesterday. None of them could remember her name, but that she looked nice because she smiled all the way through assembly, they said.

"Well, I never would have guessed it was you they were talking about," she said with a chuckle.

"Why is that June? Don't I have a nice smiling face?"

She sat down with me at the kitchen table, eager to know more about my intentions and expectations, for my new position. I had to explain that I had only been there for one day, hardly long enough to see where I would fit in best. June was my sounding board. I could talk to her openly about my hopes and fears, and know she would be supportive, but honest, in her observations. She was excited for me, and thankful her kids' school was getting a sensible person to help. As she got up from the table she remarked,

"Now then, I wonder what my kids will say when I tell them, that their new teacher is a good friend of mine, and will let me know if any of them misbehave. I can picture their faces now."

My journey to the school on my second day was not stressful at all. I was eager to get there, and uplifted by the thought that I was going to contribute to a worthy cause, by my actions, not money. Not for prestige, or status, but for practical reasons, like doing something helpful for those who needed it. I truly believe that it's not just the grand gesture that counts; it's the everyday that matters. That was my pay back, I had found my niche, and it brought me pleasure, so I sang along with the radio and smiled at the people of Lower Bridgewater.

My meeting with the Principal was very positive; she was very surprised at many of my recommendations, and said I had a true insight into the needs of the children. I tried to be guardedly optimistic about my abilities to solve some of the problems.

"Sometimes an outsider's view can clarify what has been going on under the nose of the overburdened classroom teacher. I was only watching, so it was easy for me to notice these problems, and hope I could help in the future."

"Fresh eyes are what we needed, Mary. You are an intelligent adult, with a sensible approach. We have been doing the same routine for too long, a new approach is just what we need to look at, and at least I can propose some of your ideas to the teachers, furthermore let them decide if they want to implement them, or not, in their classrooms."

I had spent hours on the internet researching and learning about the latest methodology for underachieving pupils. I now had the time and incentive to study this further.

At the end of the meeting we decided, together, that I would go into the school for two days a week, and help in the Kindergarten class where the most help was needed. The class was overcrowded with high energy pupils, and the teacher was very eager to have some assistance. I headed home, keen to start my research on the needs of a six year old.

Over dinner that night George was very talkative, of course about his own business acumen. He wasn't the least bit interested in my day, which was fine by me; I didn't want to inform him. I made polite gestures of approval, and quietly listened to his smug ranting about his competitors, when he compared them to his company.

He eventually told me what he had been leading up to. The company Daniels, Portman and Turner L.L.C. was going to open another office in Washington D.C.

"How prestigious is that Mary? James has done a splendid job of finding us just the right situation in the capital. He tells me it has a prominent address that will give us the high esteem we are looking for to get the right clients." He noticed my concerned expressions, and added,

"Don't worry, Mary, we are not moving, James and Caroline are willing to go to Washington to live and take care of business there."

I was so relieved. I managed to commend him on his company's expansion, and praised him on the progress they had made in such a short time.

"We are the movers and shakers of business Mary. Hold on to your hat, we are adding new clients' everyday." He proclaimed to me, his one and only audience.

He drank from his now customary bottle of wine with dinner, which loosened his tongue even more. Fortunately, my husband could not detect how uninterested I was in his pursuit of fame and fortune, but he tried to impress me more by speaking louder and louder. I sat bemused by his discourse, and wondered if his quest for expansion was truly a joint decision or simply, Mr. James Turner wanting to be nearer his political cronies.

"We have plans to open in New York and then into Florida in the not too distant future. I wouldn't mind the Florida office; I like the warm weather down there. What do you say, Mary?"

I couldn't answer, my mind was in shock. I wouldn't want to leave my home, my job at St John's, my trustworthy June; all were visions racing around in my head. I had only just started my new life; I didn't want to leave it. I had to ask.

"When do you think you will open these other offices?" I asked submissively.

"I can't put a time limit on that, dear. It all depends on business, we will know better after the Washington office gets up and running. Exciting though, who would have guessed a few years ago, that I was undecided about starting my own business. It just goes to show, one should always go with their gut feeling, instead of holding back."

I had the same feeling about my own venture, but it was not the time to share that with George. I told him I was happy he had made the right choice, but said I was really tired and needed to go to bed.

"Yes. Fine Mary, you toddle off, I won't be long."

He was lost in a world of his own; he was staring into his wine glass, not at me, no doubt creating in his mind, the transactions to come. I just hoped they didn't come to implementation soon; I had my own vision for the future.

I fell asleep dreaming of happy children and classrooms that were bright and cheerful. Not at all like the drab, crowded ones at St John's. I never heard George get into bed, nor did I hear him rise. Recently he had been leaving the house very early, so June had informed me. Obviously, his new company offices were where he preferred to be, with his new partners, someplace, where together they could generate a lifestyle of wealth and status in the community. These shallow, kitsch desires were not for me, I favored challenges that tested my ability to perform in difficult situations, and I had nothing in common with his new colleagues, or their new company.

I worked on my laptop all morning, enjoying my research and soaking up all the ideas and suggestions. The time flew by, until June interrupted my concentration to tell me I had a phone call from George. I was taken aback by this unusual occurrence, but I quickly picked up the extension in the study and heard George on the other end, holding two conversations at the same time.

"Yes, Glenda, tell him I will call him back straight away, I am just speaking to my wife, hallo, Mary, George here."

I tried to appear composed, as I patiently waited to learn why he would call me in the middle of the day.

"I need you to pack an overnight bag for me dear, we are going to Washington to see the new premises. I will send Glenda to pick it up. We are anticipating just one night, but it may have to be more, so put several shirts in the bag. I have some new ones in my drawer, they will be ideal. Must dash, I have a lot to do before we leave. I'll call you tomorrow. Bye Mary."

There he was again, giving orders. I would have felt better about the instructions if he had asked me to do it, not tell me. He didn't even ask me if I minded him going, or if it was convenient for me. I placed the receiver down with a bang. Shouting loudly,

"Yes, your Lordship, at your service."

June came running into the room asking if I was O.K. and hoping it wasn't bad news from Mr. Daniels.

"Actually, it is good news, as far as I am concerned. Mr. Daniels needs a bag to be packed. He is going out of town for a few days." I nastily said. "Could you spare a little time to help me?"

Of course, dependable June didn't ask any more questions, and followed me upstairs. She gathered toiletries together, while I packed his clothes and underwear into the bag. When we had finished she offered to make me a sandwich and a pot of coffee, as I looked like I needed some sustenance.

Later that afternoon Ms. Glenda arrived for the suitcase. I took it to the door, but did not ask her in. Very courtly, I handed her the suitcase containing my husband's personal belongings. It felt like I was giving her a portion of George, offering it over with no questions asked, although I did wonder if she was going along with the partners on the trip. I quickly decided to reject this jealous thought; I certainly wouldn't have gone with them to Washington, even if I had been asked. I had more important matters to attend to.

George going out of town enabled me to use my time, how I wanted to, on my personal desires, without being accountable to George or feeling guilty for deceiving him.

I spent the rest of the week going to the library, or visiting children's bookstores and researching more web sites for ideas. I was fully absorbed in this venture, and wanted to be fully prepared and committed when my services were needed.

Over the weekend, George called to say he was expanding his stay in the capital, as more possibilities had emerged, which he wanted to pursue. He didn't ask about my well-being, nor did he ask me if I minded. The message was given to me as fait accompli and didn't warrant discussion, so I replied,

"O.K. George just let me know, when to expect you home. Take care."

"Of course, dear, speak to you soon," was his response.

JUDY SERVENTI

# Chapter 12
# The Unknown World

I started at the school the following week, armed with the knowledge I had learned of what a Kindergarten child's needs were likely to be, but none of it prepared me for the reality.

The children were noisy and unruly, but somehow Miss Glass, the teacher, managed to get their attention, well most of them, for some of the time. At the break, I ask her if I could make a suggestion, to which she had no objection. From my research I found an article about Kindergarten classes who sat on the floor, rather than at their desks for some of the time. She was willing to try that. The problem was the wooden floors were not comfortable, and they were very old.

My solution was to make a corner of the room into a reading area. I brought in some throw rugs and pillows from home and borrowed big picture books from the library. Slowly but surely my first proposal materialized, and became a success over the following weeks. Reading to the class gave me as much pleasure as it seemed to give to the children.

Another duty of mine, on the days I was there, was to accompany the children into assembly. I didn't mind at all doing this, however, I was puzzled by where Miss Glass went with one little girl, while assembly was taking place. I was curious to find out the reason, but was shocked by the explanation.

The little girl, Martha, came from a really poor family. She had to be washed and changed from her own clothes before coming into the classroom. This had to be done to get rid of the smell, so other children would accept her. Miss Glass said, she had managed to keep the head lice at bay, but needed to change her clothes every morning.

When I asked more about this child from the Principal, she informed me that they couldn't send Martha home in the clothes provided for her, because her parents would sell them, or exchange them for other things. So the routine was, she was washed and changed every morning, and then changed again at the end of the day.

This was one of the tasks I was willing to do for Miss Glass; however, I was not ready for the subsequent occurrences. I had taken Martha's hand and led her to the bathrooms. She looked up at me with a face too small to hold the bad black teeth she smiled with. The odor from her was turning over my stomach, but I gripped her tightly and spoke to her tenderly.

"Do you mind if I help you this morning?" I asked her softly.

"No Miss, I like it when I get clean."

I didn't pry into her life by asking anything more. I gently removed her tatty shoes and clothes and washed her. A special box had been given to me by the Principal, with the necessary toiletries and fresh clothes. Silently, I started the task. I removed her shabby dress and her under vest, and then I noticed the red marks along her back. I had never seen whip marks, or injuries from punishment so I couldn't identify the cause.

I hesitantly asked Martha if they hurt, but she shook her head and said they didn't. After returning her to the classroom, I decided to see Miss Jenkins, and report to her what I had seen. She told me that Miss Glass had also reported the matter to her, but she was reluctant to make an allegation to the Social Services just yet.

"Mary, will you come with me to Martha's home and maybe we can speak to the parents, to find out what is going on?"

I certainly wanted to find out, and so we both got into my car to drive to the address. Nothing could have primed me for that visit. It was a world I had never seen. The address was in a tenement building, but the window at that address had a dirty cloth across it instead of glass. The paint on the door was peeling off, and the door was held upright by one hinge.

We knocked and waited, listening to the wails of children inside. Eventually a small heavily pregnant woman appeared, carrying a baby, and with two other toddlers hanging on to her legs.

Miss Jenkins introduced us and told her briefly that we were not the Social Services, but from St John's where her daughter Martha was a pupil.

"Oh, has there been some trouble, is my Martha O.K.?" she asked.

My friend consoled her, and then asked if we could go inside rather than talk on the doorstep. Reluctantly she let us in, informing us that her husband was not at home, but out looking for work. The reek of the inside, made me gasp, but I tried to keep my composure, and took out my handkerchief to wipe my nose.

She put down the baby on the sofa that was shiny with grease and dirt, asking us if we would like something to drink, which of course we declined. Then, Barbara asked about the marks we had found on Martha's back. The Mother quickly responded,

"We might be poor, but we've never put a finger on any of our kids, me and my husband love em too much for that. No, no, never. Did our Martha tell you we did?" she pleaded.

Barbara, explained that her daughter had not said they did, but that it looked suspicious. Then she cautiously suggested that maybe she could get some help, and assistance for them.

"I think I know where I could find some help for you, but I must have a full picture of your necessities. Can you show us around?"

"Well, there's not much to see, this room, a kitchen and one bedroom."

She led us through to the bedroom. The door wouldn't open; something seemed to be blocking it, so we both pushed hard. It was a red woolen coat. There was just one bed covered by dirty sheets.

"How do you all sleep in this room?" Barbara asked.

"Well we can't all get in the bed, so some of the kids have to sleep on the floor." She indicated to the red woolen coat.

Barbara reached down to inspect it, and then she turned to the Mother and told her, with sincerity, she would get help for her as soon as she could. We left in silence, waving as we got into the car in a gesture of kindness and compassion, which we hoped it conveyed.

On the journey home I questioned why we had left so abruptly, when we hadn't got the real truth from the Mother.

"Yes we did, Mary," she said, " the red coat was soaked in urine, and if Martha was sleeping on that, with the other toddlers, then the stains on her back were burned into her skin by the red dye and urine, I must get help for that family."

I was speechless, that such poverty could exist. There were more problems besides trying to teach and learn going on at St John's.

# Chapter 13
# Big Business

That trip to the capital, my husband made was not a short one, it was two full weeks. Not that I was really concerned, but he felt it necessary to bore me with the details.

They had a 'Grand Opening' for the new office, and sent out invitations to all the prominent people in the city. They invited high-flyers, politicians and the media. They also extended the invitations to include an extra guest of their choice. Apparently, this was a gimmick that James Turner had used before.

"Mary, you can't envisage the crowd we had," he said shaking his head. "We never imagined the response we got. They overflowed into the corridor, and as people left, more people arrived. We decided that it was impossible to talk to each person, individually, so James stood on a chair and gave a sort of mini lecture outlining our business projects, as well as how they could benefit from our services. What a day, Mary, you should have been there to see it."

I think his last remark was a rhetorical question said to keep my interest, but he continued anyway with further descriptions of the event. Apparently, Glenda was amazing giving out cards at the door as they left. Well. I wouldn't have expected anything less, I sarcastically thought to myself. Noting she was in fact there, in Washington. I had to ask.

"Who ran the office here while you all were in Washington?"

His answer was equally surprising to me. Apparently they had increased their office staff, also hiring an office manager some weeks before. He added that they all were extremely qualified either in finance or corporate law. An extended stay in Washington had become necessary for the partners to cope with the increased business, and help James hire the right staff to take over when he returned.

"It's very easy to keep in touch from afar with the new technology, Mary; I spoke to our people here everyday."

I smiled in response to hide my resentment, because I had not had a daily update from him, either by telephone, Skype or even a fax from his 'amazing secretary'.

"Now we have established a pattern of opening new offices, we all feel confident we can expand our business further." He gestured with his long sweeping arms to exaggerate his statement.

I listened all that evening about his desires for the future, and not one of them was debatable. As I went to bed that night I was angry, confused and bewildered at the same time, not knowing how I was going to assimilate into my husband's life.

I was contented that one of his partners, James Turner, was working in Washington. I had an uneasy, gut feeling, about him from the beginning, Glenda, his secretary, I had met only twice, but again I thought she was arrogant, to say the least. However, Brad Portman, I did like. He was the eldest of the three partners. His mature good looks added to his demeanor, his politeness and good manners were quiet and unpretentious.

When Brad asked George to join his Gentleman's Club, I had no qualms about it, and that kind of social commitment gave George pleasure, so I encouraged him to go.

The two of them went to sporting events together; apparently they had a company box in every activity, baseball, basketball, football, tennis and even horse racing. These male only leisure activities, suited my husband, and they gave me the time to spend on my projects.

Frequently, they both appeared in the newspaper, or on the television news channels shaking hands with the managers or players. I only knew this, because George would buy the newspaper to show me, or make sure we watched the right channel that evening, really for him to gloat over his popularity. This, in truth, didn't impress me, but if that kind of shallow esteem made him happy, then so be it, I thought to myself.

"I wish you would accompany me to some of these social events, Mary, I could buy you a new wardrobe and then you would realize that you would be wearing the finest dresses and jewels in the room. Every woman I know would jump at the chance to own these trinkets. What's wrong with you, woman?" he bellowed at me.

His shouting would result in me crying, and then my sobs would cause him to yell more, before he left the room disgusted at my ungratefulness. This was always followed the next day by large bouquets of flowers with a 'sorry' note attached.

"I know you love me, George," I would try to explain, "but I don't feel comfortable at your social events, and I don't want to be a wall-flower, or to dress in finery to impress people I don't know. I am more at ease spending my time having lunch with my friend, going to bookstores, libraries and art stores." I added, stretching the truth. "Please let me enjoy my leisure time in my own way, and you carry on doing what gives you pleasure. Just explain my absence in a way that suits the occasion, I am sure you can do that."

Although I was apologizing, he seemed to understand the logic behind my harsh words. He accepted my negative response to his suggestions by saying,

"Well, they would also be a good investment. I suppose, whether you wear them or not."

I was glad he had found his own solution to the situation, and the concession he found suited us both. We had come to a compromise that we both were satisfied with. George admitted to me that he would be bored to tears going to museums, art galleries and bookstores, and that I should carry on going to these places with my friend. He added that if I wanted to buy some artwork or needed extra cash to purchase anything, he would make sure there was enough money in our joint account to do this.

I did enjoy going to these places on the days I was not at the school. I purchased some storybooks for the children, took pictures at the art shows, and picked up brochures at the museums. These children no doubt would never get to see these exhibitions; however, I thought it might be possible for me to organize a field trip, but the logistics of that I knew, I would have to discuss with Barbara, the Principal.

# Chapter 14
## Dealing with Problems

My days and weeks at St John's flew by; I was so wrapped up in my vocation. Miss Glass and I worked well together, also, the children seemed to like our different approaches to teaching. There was never time for them to be bored or disinterested in learning.

Little by little, my time at the school was increased. I had no regrets about spending my time there. June was taking care of the house, the laundry and the occasional grocery shopping, so I was free to extend my hours.

I moved up the grade levels, and experienced how different their needs were. It was during my time with a 4th Grade class that I met Tommy. He was small for his age, and like Martha, he was under-nourished, shabby and dirty.

Unfortunately, he demanded my full attention. As I moved around the classroom helping other children, he would be by my side. If I talked to a child for too long, he would put his hands on my cheeks, and turn my face to his. The teacher seemed to be quite happy with the arrangement of him being tethered to me, as long as I didn't mind.

She explained that he was the eldest of ten children, and he was only ten. He was obviously seeking attention and affection, something he probably never got at home. My heart went out to him.

He had another trait that was not good. Barbara told me he had been lighting fires in derelict buildings, in the sheds and waste bins outside his house. The fire brigade had been called so many times that they had reported the events to the authorities. The parents had been sent warnings that they could be liable for restitution, and the whole business was escalating. It seems that the fires occur after something had upset Tommy. His Father was known to be violent with his wife, and even with the children, which affected Tommy immensely. Maybe Tommy's Father had punished him because they didn't have any money to pay a fine, Barbara had speculated.

"Does he know it is wrong to light fires?" I asked

"Well, when I asked him that question he told me he did know it was wrong, but he liked to watch the flames go up into the air, that made him happy."

In the weeks following my conversation with Barbara the inevitable happened. The news hit the newspapers and television. The janitor at the school had yelled at Tommy for loitering outside after the school bell had rung, and that evening the janitor's office went up in flames. Luckily the small building was separate from the main school building, so the fire was contained, and the janitor had returned home at the end of the day, so consequently no one was inside.

Tommy was seen by a local outside the school just before the janitor's office went up in flames. The person told the authorities that the boy did not run away, but stood watching the fire until the fire brigade appeared. That person knew Tommy's family well, so could identify him.

I felt helpless as the wheels of justice turned against Tommy. They had two alternatives because of his age. One was to detain him as a ward of the state for psychological treatment, or keep him under close supervision by a case worker, who would give him counseling. They chose to make him a ward of state, and take him away from his family, because of Tommy's home situation.

I cried myself to sleep for numerous nights, silently sobbing as my husband lay beside me, oblivious of my indescribable reason. His life held no similarities that he could compare with, nor would he have the compassion to understand my distress. The void between us was widening.

Our separate lifestyles suited us both. I refrained from asking questions about his work, and he rarely asked how I had spent my day. Mealtimes were taken apart from each other, mainly because of his work schedule. George attended more and more luncheons, business dinners and spent more late nights at work. I ate when I came home from school. Weekends, when we should have had time together were the occasions for George to attend football or baseball matches, not at all my favorite pastimes.

I developed more of a friendship with Barbara, as we had similar tastes in leisure and pleasure. We went to the theater, to the cinema or to book signings. We would have lunch together, and talk endlessly about solutions to the problems at St John's. I was at ease with Barbara, and therefore, she could ask me personal questions without offending me, and she did.

"Are you and George still a married couple, does he come home to you every evening?"

It was awkward for me to explain why George and I didn't go out much together. The excuses that he was working, or that he was out of town, became implausible. When she asked me if George came home, and if our relationship was still good, I found myself searching for the reality. I could say with sincerity that we shared the same bed, and when he was not at the Washington office he came home every night, but I was not willing to share even with Barbara, my intimate details.

However, this conversation did make me realize I had to put more effort into saving our marriage. I had been preoccupied with my new venture since the loss of our baby. Sex before had always been a means to an end for me. I wanted a family. Then when it became clear that was not going to happen, I lost the desire to make love. I pondered if indeed George felt the same way. He had told me many times that he was so tired these days that he could fall asleep as soon as his head reached the pillow. I had also been so worn-out after a day at school that a soft kiss on the cheek, before we switched off the light, had been sufficient for me. I concluded that this was a conversation I needed to have with George.

That day was appropriate, it was our wedding anniversary, so I decided to make a nice dinner, open a bottle of wine and then perhaps we could spend a pleasant evening together talking. I had made this suggestion to George the week before to give him plenty notice, and he seemed to be all for it. Fortunately, the date was on Friday, the end of the work week, and this fitted into his work schedule.

I prepared, with June's help, a three course meal of all his favorite dishes, and before June left she had set the dining room table with all our best china, and a centerpiece of fresh flowers. I expected George to come home early that day, and hoped we could eat about 7 o' clock. The food was ready for that time frame.

I made an extra effort to dress for dinner. Putting on my reliable black dress and a necklace, hoping this would set the scene for an evening of pleasure. I poured myself a cocktail, which was not my usual start to an evening, but I needed false courage to carry out my plan. I wanted George to give me mad passionate sex, the kind we both fanatically participated in before my pregnancy.

7 o'clock came and went, then 7.30p.m was showing on my watch. I rang his office, but no one answered. I called his cell, and waited. He answered,

"Oh, Mary dear, I am so sorry. Things became rather hectic at the end of the day, and I am on my way home. I've just called at the florist for a bunch of flowers for you and Glenda kindly picked up your present for me, so I will be with you shortly. Pour me a whisky, dear, I need it."

I gulped down my drink in aggravation. Surely he could have passed on his workload to an employee for one day, and why must his secretary be involved in our gift giving? I looked at the table setting of fresh cut flowers. I didn't need more. I wanted my husband, not his presents and flowers. Disgusted, I poured his whisky and another cocktail for myself, trying to compose myself for his arrival. This was not the way I wanted the evening to start; George's capricious actions were dampening my libido just when I was searching to get it back.

George walked into the room clutching the flowers, and an expensive looking gift box. He handed them to me saying,

"Take these from me dear, then I can get this overcoat off and loosen my tie, it's been one hell of a day,"

I took the gifts, and waited for the greeting. He quickly took off his coat and his tie, and threw them on the sofa, then said,

"Where's my drink, Mary, did you pour it with very little ice?"

Silently, I placed the flowers and box next to his coat, and obediently went to the cabinet where I had left his glass; the ice had already melted so I just added one ice cube to the mix. Needless to say he gulped it down in one.

"I'll hang your coat up, and put the flowers in water. Are you ready to eat right away?" I quietly asked, noticing he was pouring another whisky into his glass.

I hung up his coat in the hallway, and then went through into the kitchen. I left the flowers in the sink, and then took the appetizers into the dining room.

The evening had started badly, however, there was time to reverse this, and I was trying sincerely hard to stay optimistic. I didn't want to rush things along. We sat together eating our appetizers George loved, in silence. The tranquil atmosphere was feeling too quiet, so I asked George to please open the red wine that I had set aside on the drink cabinet, while I went for the main course.

By the time I had plated and brought in the dinner, George was drinking his wine.

"I don't like you rushing in and out Mary, bringing in the dinner, I could have arranged a catering company to come in and cook and serve us. It is a special occasion after all."

I tried to explain that this approach of home cooking in an intimate setting suited me better, but he apparently he could not see it my way. I struggled to keep up with him drinking the wine in an endeavor to calm myself. However, after the second bottle I was without doubt not succeeding. I brought in the dessert, but by now I was unable to digest it. Nevertheless, George was happy to finish my share as well.

"You are going to pile on weight, eating so much, George, be careful at those functions you go to, and pace yourself." I said with a smile.

"I don't eat so much when I am there, but this meal tonight Mary, surpasses any food I've had in ages. I must admit a caterer could not have reached this standard. Every plate has been delicious, so let me be excessive tonight," he answered, helping himself to more.

The night was getting better, and I was relaxed enough to say,

"We should do this more often then, at least once a week, I think would be a good idea."

He didn't answer me, or he ignored my suggestion. Instead he offered to open some champagne while I opened my present. He assured me there was some in the wine cooler cabinet in the kitchen that was waiting for a special occasion.

He came back with the crystal glasses and the large bottle of renowned champagne. With a gesture of finesse he corked the champagne and poured it gently into the glasses, handing one to me, then he lifted his glass in the air to toast our anniversary,

"I have the most wonderful wife in the world. May we have many more years together!" He said the words loud and distinctly, as though he was speaking to an audience, not just to me. I lifted my glass and said quietly, but genuinely,

"Cheers."

He sat down and leaned his elbows on the table cupping the glass, and asked me to open my present. I retrieved it from the sofa where I had left it, and brought it to the table. I delicately took apart the expensive wrapping paper, fearful of the contents, and trying hard not to spoil the evening by showing my disgust for reckless spending.

Inside the box was the most elaborate string of diamonds I had ever seen. Each stone was surrounded by rubies, and there were over twelve stones on the chain. I had seen pictures of European Queens and Princesses at the museum wearing such jewelry, but I never thought I would touch such gems.

George was watching me carefully as he poured more champagne into his glass. I was frozen to my seat, I was embarrassed by the extravagance, but tried to suppress my repulsion at the opulence. I attempted to fain a good response, but the words would not come out.

"There you are Mary, I knew you would be speechless, they are a very rare find that my jeweler managed to acquire. Let me put them round your neck so you can see for yourself what fine stones do for your already pretty eyes.

With a great deal of difficulty he got up from his chair, and put the priceless object around my neck. I felt I had to participate in the charade to please him, in order to keep my hopes of pleasure later.

I touched them as I looked at my reflection in the mirror. They were cold, sharp and shiny, not warm and friendly like my beloved fake pearls. I told George they were a wonderful gift, and I loved him so much. For the first time in ages we kissed ardently, holding the embrace. My erotic desires had been rekindled.

I gently took off the necklace and put it back into the box, where it truly belonged. We both returned to the table where George changed his drink to cognac, turning the glass round in his hands and sipping his favorite nectar.

Finally we went upstairs together. I went into the bathroom to put on the flimsy nightdress I had last worn on our honeymoon. I took off my makeup and applied a small amount of perfume to my hair. I went through the door jubilant, ready to make love, and make up for missed time, only to see my husband in a deep sleep and to hear him snoring loudly.

# Chapter 15
# Forgive and Forget

The following morning was Saturday. It was a free day for me, but I didn't know if George had somewhere to go. I awoke early, and went downstairs to clear away the dishes and glasses from our anniversary dinner.

I filled the dishwasher and was clearing the final things from the table, when George appeared bleary eyed at the door, still in his robe and pajamas.

"I'm a little fuzzy this morning, Mary. I think I will go back to bed for a little longer, don't make any breakfast for me." He turned from the door to go back upstairs, not waiting for me to reply.

By his appearance and demeanor, I don't think he had any clear recollections of our anniversary dinner. If he did, he wasn't apologizing for anything, that was certain.

I made a pot of coffee for myself, and as I sat at the kitchen table I remembered the good and the unfortunate events of the previous evening. I knew my husband's intentions were true, but his ideals of what made me happy had really missed the mark. Fancy presents and superfluous words were not what I wanted.

Later that morning, George surfaced from his lie in, looking a whole lot better. He had showered and put on some casual clothes that I had never seen before, but I had to admit, he looked handsome and affluent.

We ate a light breakfast together, so we could eventually have a conversation. I thanked him for my present, but added that I would feel more comfortable if it was in a safe, either in our home or at his office, until the right time came to wear it.

"Well, we don't have a safe here, unless I get one, but I do have one at the office," he answered, "if that makes you feel better." he added mystified by my concerns.

"It's just that I am on edge leaving such expensive jewelry in my dressing table drawer." I explained.

"No problem, dear. Do you still have the box you can pack them into, if not, I will get one from my jeweler friend."

"I think it would be more appropriate for him to supply the box for such a special group of items. I will pack them, before you take them to the office."

I was pleased with that arrangement. I could never imagine myself wearing such an ostentatious necklace, nor any of the other pretentious pieces George wanted to purchase. He seemed quite content with the safekeeping part of my argument, so I was relieved from the pressure, for the time being.

The rest of the weekend we spent no differently than usual, George going to a football match with Brad, and I was left to my own devises, my attempt at reconciliation ending in a stalemate. My only regret was that I knew I still had deep feelings for my husband, yet he was evidently in a world of his own. I decided to accept this fact, and absorb myself in my fulfilling occupation.

Monday could not arrive too soon for me, I was anxious to see another grade level. This grade was their final year at the school before going on to Junior High. Before I joined this class, Barbara gave me the background to them.

She explained that these children, although most of them were only eleven or twelve years old, acted like they were young adults. Disciplining them was difficult; they took charge of their younger siblings at home because of absent parents, and so thought they had all the answers in life.

She believed they were the fodder for the street gangs in Lower Bridgewater; they were tempted at every street corner to join a group that offered them a better life than sitting in a classroom. Temptation, along with apathetic parents, led a good number of them to go astray. Mr. Price was their teacher, and he definitely needed assistance in his classroom.

I watched this class in assembly many times, and noticed their teacher kept control of them in a regimental manner. His girls came in first, followed by the boys. They seemed to be reconciled to his approach, because I never noticed any of them being badly behaved.

I was curious, knowing their backgrounds, how he managed this control, and I was soon to find out. There were around 28 children in his class, an equal mixture of boys and girls. I had no idea of what a regular 12 year old looked like, but this group certainly gave me the impression that they appeared to be older than twelve.

Their teacher told me it was because they had experienced more than the average child of their age group encounters, and this awareness was shown in their speech, mannerisms and appearance. He also confided in me, and told me he knew this to be true because he had grown up in Lower Bridgewater. It was only when he left to go to college did he realize how insular his outlook on life and people had been.

As I watched him teach, I pondered on the reason the children listened to him. He was one of them, he could be trusted, and he gave them hope for their own future dreams. His classroom set up was different from others I had seen. He sat them in a semi-circle with his desk on a wall at the side. He stood in the middle of the semi- circle as he taught; only leaving it to write on the blackboard or talk to an individual child who needed his attention.

He spoke to them in a quiet, but sincere voice using his fingers and his arms to emphasize the point he was making. He was always moving, even when the class was writing, he seemed to manage to go to each child, checking or explaining to them if they had not clearly understood the lesson.

I was in awe of Mr. Price. I had sat at the back of his class, behind the children so I wouldn't be a distraction, but he regularly brought me into his discussions, for a corroboration of his statements. I was privileged to be part of this man's teaching abilities.

I was not sure how I could be of help in his class; he seemed to have everything under control. Nevertheless I asked if he needed me to do anything.

He was genuinely pleased to have some help. He explained to me that not all of the children were at the same academic level, in fact, some were way behind, and needed extra individual help to increase their levels before their tests at the end of the year. He assured me he would give me his lesson notes the day before, so I could make sure I understood what he wanted from me, and he would always be around to clarify things.

So, I found myself studying at night, and tutoring during the day. I sat at his desk while he taught, and then when the children did the exercises, I took the ones who needed extra help to the desk, to work with them.

It was during one of these sessions that I first met Florence. Recently she had fainted in assembly, and I had gone to her assistance, then again that morning, she had fainted once more. I discreetly helped her up, and took her outside to get some fresh air. We sat on a bench outside, where, I hoped she would confide in me. I asked if she had eaten breakfast, thinking that may be the reason she was fainting.

"No, Miss, I feel too sick in the mornings to eat." She replied sheepishly.

"Are you having a bad time of the month, Florence? Have you started your periods yet?"

"Yes I did start them, but now I've stopped. I've not seen one for ages."

"Florence, do you think you could be pregnant?" I tentively asked, trying not to sound shocked.

"Dunno, Miss, I hope not." She answered nonchalantly.

I held both her hands and told her I was there to help, but she reacted unexpectedly, and pushed my hands away. She stood up and ran for the bathrooms screaming,

"You can't help, nobody can, leave me alone."

My first impulse was to follow her into the bathrooms, but instead I decided to talk the matter over with Barbara. Unfortunately, Barbara was at a meeting and not in school that day, so I went looking for Florence.

I looked under each door until I saw her foot standing on what I thought was blood. There wasn't a lot of blood, only small drips. I knocked on the door.

"Florence," I called softly, "its Mrs. Daniels, please come out, I will keep your secret, please, let me help you."

I waited, but she stayed inside. I tried again to persuade her.

"You're bleeding, Florence, come out and let me fix it for you."

She was crying and whimpering, as if she was in pain. I was getting fearful of what was happening behind the closed door, and I was just going to try to force it open, when Florence came out holding her arm. I was confused, but she went to the sink to wash away the blood, and I followed.

"Were you cutting yourself, Florence?" I said, as I reached for the paper towels. She nodded her head. I held my hand out, hoping she would hand over the offending tool. Florence reached into her pocket and retrieved a razor blade, which she willingly put on my palm.

"I'm sorry Miss, I know it's wrong, am I in real trouble now with the Principal?"

"Florence, you have to trust me. I can help you, if you will let me."

We walked together outside, and went back to the bench. She was visibly shaking, plus I knew she needed some food and a hot drink. I told her not to move, and I would return in a few minutes.

I went to the secretary's office and told her I was taking Florence home, as she had been sick, and moreover she also had fainted earlier.

"Half of these kids don't get a breakfast before they come to school, that's the problem. Their parents would rather spend their money on booze instead of food," she said dispassionately,

I asked for Florence's address before I filled in the necessary paper work to release her from school, then I returned to the bench. Luckily, she was still there, holding her arm, and rocking to and fro. I told her I was going to take her home, but to my surprise she refused.

"No, Miss, please don't take me home. I don't want my Mother to know anything. She's got a lot on her plate, and she doesn't know. I'm not going home. Not ever. I'll stay here; I'll not be a bother, honestly. I feel a lot better now, I'll go back to class, but don't tell Mr. Price about me cutting, will you?"

I explained that I had signed her out of school, and we could go together somewhere to have a warm drink. I agreed I would not take her home if that was what she wanted. We walked together to my car. I switched on the heating and wrapped the car rug around her. She had told me she didn't want to sit in front in case somebody recognized her, so she lay along the back seat under the rug.

I drove around Lower Bridgewater looking for a café, but couldn't find one. I asked Florence if she knew where there was one, and realized she had fallen asleep in the warm car.

My inclination was to drive to my house, but I was not sure how June would react to me bringing home a child from school. However, my fears were set aside as my Mothering nurture took over.

I confidently woke Florence up, and explained I had brought her to my house for a hot lunch.

She was too bewildered to resist, and with the car rug still wrapped around her, I ushered her through the door. I explained to June, who was in the kitchen, about Florence fainting at school, and that she was feeling unwell.

June asked no questions, and quickly had a hot drink and a bowl of hot soup on the table in no time at all. Florence relished the soup and sipped the hot tea while fearfully watching June. I asked if she wanted more soup, and she eagerly pushed the empty bowl forward with a nod of her head.

Still wrapped in the rug her injured arm could not be seen, and she was noticeably conscious of hiding it from June. I wanted to clean and bandage it. When she had finished the second bowl I asked her if she wanted to use the toilet. This enabled me to take her into my bathroom to attend to her cuts. When I finished, I suggested she lie down in my spare bedroom, until she felt better. She didn't resist, and snuggled down quickly, still dressed, on the bed. I covered her with the duvet and left the room.

When I returned to the kitchen, June informed me that she knew Florence and her family, so she would return her home when Florence woke up.

All the information June gave me was wrapped up in a few simple words.

"That's a real bad family, the pits."

# Chapter 16
# Bigotry and Conceit

A few days later my husband informed me that he wanted me to accompany him to New York. We were to leave the following morning. The company was going to open another office there, and Brad and Vicky Portman needed our help.

"Vicky wants you to assist her in finding a home while I help Brad with the new office. We have done this before, so it shouldn't be too hard for us to follow the same format; however, it doesn't give him the time to help Vicky find a place." He rambled on, leaving no time for questions or objections. "It's the least you can do, dear, and it will be a nice vacation for you. We could fit in a Broadway show, and see the sights. Just pack what you can; you can shop for more outfits when you get there, the choices will be more appropriate in New York than here."

He wasn't going to take no, for an answer, but I didn't want to leave so quickly. St John's needed me more than Vicky Portman, I was sure. George had the flights and the hotel booking, and even a car to pick us up to go to the airport. I had to call Barbara to explain.

Fortunately, she was very supportive saying,

"I wish I had a husband who could whisk me off to New York City in a flash, just bring us back some souvenirs and pictures to show the children. Have fun, we'll miss you."

I put the receiver down with tears in my eyes, knowing I would miss them more. I packed my bag, confused if I had chosen the right clothes for the 'big apple', but in truth not caring. If I was being judged by my wardrobe, then so be it.

The limousine came, and we were whisked away, in style, to the airport, where we boarded first class to join Brad and Vicky already on board. They were comfortably sipping on the courtesy champagne, and George quickly joined them. I wanted to decline, as it was too early in the day for me, but George would have none of it.

"Come on, Mary, enjoy the fruits of my labor," he pompously said aloud.

That kind of behavior from George was going to be the norm; I could feel it from the start. We arrived at J.F.K. and then took a taxi to the hotel, none other than the Waldorf Astoria. My husband was in his glory, ordering the porters around, but giving large, super large, tips. I sat back as he went to the reception, requesting all sorts of services. We followed the porter to the elevator, and finally to our room, well, not exactly a room, but a suite. I was shocked by the lavishness.

"Can we really afford such luxury, George?" I asked naively.

"We are on company business, and therefore, on company expense. Enjoy it, for heaven's sake, Mary, relax," he said with vehemence.

I thought of Barbara's parting words, and decided I should count my blessings, and enjoy myself. I asked George to order a pot of tea and some sandwiches while I took a shower.

"That's more like it, now you are getting into the swing of things. Remember, we are meeting Brad and Vicky for dinner tonight, I hope you have brought something suitable?" He shouted through to the bathroom. "We are eating here in the dining room, it's more convenient,"

As I showered I smiled, and thought about my reliable black dress I had packed as an after thought. I was sure they wouldn't remember it if I added my colorful silk scarf around my neck.

I did just that, and thankfully George did not discern my outfit was not new, as other issues were on his mind.

"Mary I have forgotten to bring your jewelry box, what a shame, shall I send a message for Glenda to get it to us somehow?"

I told him it wasn't necessary, and that I thought the trip to New York was a house-hunting venture, not a string of social evenings. Thankfully, he was persuaded by my remark, and the jewelry box matter was dropped.

My time in New York was eventually exciting. I had accompanied Vicky to see several houses outside the city, large monstrosities, which to me would be a lot of wasted space for just the two of them, and would take an awful lot of heating with the cathedral ceilings they all had. Thankfully she employed a realtor, and so I was free to go my own way.

I began with what, for me, was the real place to start in New York, the Statue of Liberty. I went on the ferry and saw what the turn of the century immigrants saw as they approached the New World. I continued on the ferry to Ellis Island where they were processed. I remembered to pick up post cards and a film to show the students on my return.

The days were going too fast for me then; George had booked for only one week. I wandered round the Museum of Modern Art, Rockefeller

Center, the 9/11 Memorial, picking up all the literature I could for the children who might never see these places.

In the evening when we went to a Broadway show, I was astounded by Times Square and the street artists. George was so busy he didn't know if I was with Vicky or not, and she was quite happy to let me see the sights that she had seen many times before.

At the end of that glorious week I was elated, and eager to share my experiences with the pupils. I had to purchase an extra wheelie case to carry all my souvenirs. My husband assumed I had been shopping for a new wardrobe of clothes, so I didn't inform him otherwise.

On the plane back home he remarked how well I looked after the trip, he told me the shopping in the big city had evidently brought me pleasure.
"Now we have offices in New York and Washington you can go shopping more often. You don't need to wait for me to go along with you; the company expenses can be made available to cover any visit. Glenda will arrange everything; just tell her when you want to go."

I lay back and slept, dreaming of my presentations I could give to St John's.

# Chapter 17
# Putting it into Perspective

June was my first audience to hear about my New York activities, which she relished, as much as I did experiencing them. She suggested I should invite some of the parents to the presentation, as she knew of many who would attend, if they could bring their younger children with them.

Thinking of parents and children reminded me of Florence, as a result I asked about the time she had taken her home.

"Were the parents in when you got there?"

"They were in alright; I could hear the yelling and screaming before we got out of the car. Apparently, one of the siblings had told their Dad that Florence had left school with a woman; consequently, when I turned up they thought it was me. I didn't want to expand on their assumptions so I just told them; she had fainted, and was sick. I told them nobody was in at their house when I first called, and they accepted my account."

June went on to say that the Father was very anxious to know what Florence had been saying.

He said Florence was full of lies, so whatever she had talked about was all in her imagination.

"Now, I wonder why he was curious to know if she had told things to us?" I asked. "She is pregnant you know, June. Perhaps they are keeping it hushed up because of her age?"

"I thought as much. I put two and two together in the car on our way to her house and I asked who the Father was?"

"Did she tell you?"

"Well, yes, but you won't believe it." June paused, and then watching my face carefully, she responded, "Mr. Price."

I couldn't help my mouth opening without any words coming out. I sat down at the kitchen table to try and take in this information.

"Surely, she's lying, why is she being so deceitful?" I questioned, trying to get my head around her accusation. "Is she covering up for someone else? It could be any of the boys in Lower Bridgewater; she does look and act a lot older than she is."

We talked it over together, and June associated many of the times she had seen Florence and her friend, hanging around with the wrong set of teenage boys.

"When you're a teenager you need to have loving parents who monitor and control the time spent out of school. My lot says I give them no leeway at all, but that's how it has to be in our area."

I agreed, even though I had no children of my own, I could look back on my own strict upbringing, and thank them for it.

"Do you think I should tell Mr. Price about what Florence is saying?" I asked, apprehensively.

June was shaking her head before I had finished the question, and I was relieved she felt the same way. I had to talk to Florence, myself, and see if I get the same story. This whole matter was getting out of hand, and whoever the Father was, Florence was going to be a Mother.

I drove to school the next Monday morning, observing more intently the boys on the street corners. To me, some of them didn't look old enough to be out of school, but nevertheless, they were smoking, laughing, and enjoying their time on the street.

I brought the matter up with Barbara, and asked if anyone monitored the boys if they were absent from school. She told me that at the High School the situation was uncontrollable. The authorities would take the parents to court and fine them, but the parents had no money, so it was a revolving door situation.

I also mentioned the matter to Mr. Price during our break time, and he had a different opinion. He told me it was a 'rite of passage' in Lower Bridgewater, for the boys to hang around the street corners.

"Remember Ms. Daniels, this is a different culture. They are learning their own values and beliefs, their social hierarchies are being established, and their own social status recognized. To many observers this is an alien life, but for them it is status quo."

I had to remind myself that this was Mr. Price's 'home turf', and his insight into the area's traditions was first-hand. I did note, however, that his explanation sounded uncompromising and abrasive. I had never heard him use this dictatorial approach with his students; perhaps he did see me as an outsider after all.

I decided to observe the class more closely. I watched the interaction between Florence and Mr. Price, and it was very friendly. He praised her, for getting the correct answer to a problem by patting the back of her hand. She looked up to him with worshipful eyes, which he seemed to ignore.

The boys in the class had a reverence for him that he arrogantly accepted, and most of the girls treated him like a pop star, vying for his individual attention. The seating arrangement that I had found so appealing when I first saw it, changed in my mind to be his theatrical stage.

I pondered the accusation from Florence in my mind, and came to the conclusion that it could only be a fabrication of the truth. He was an excellent teacher, who seemed to genuinely care for all of the children in his class.

During the break time I asked Florence if I could speak to her privately. Mr. Price had gone to the staff room, and all the other children were heading outside. I first asked her how she was feeling, if she was still being sick or had fainted again. She looked at me nervously,

"No, Miss, I'm feeling fine now."

I delicately inquired if her periods had returned, but she looked at the ground, and told me, that they hadn't, but her Mother had told her it was normal for a girl of her age to have irregular periods.

I knew it was useless to ask if she had seen a Doctor, so, I asked her to remember I would always be around, if she needed help.

As the weeks went by I watched Florence closely, and when I was giving her individual attention, I always began by asking how she was feeling. My question was posed in a matter of fact way, as most people say in a greeting. However, Florence took it differently.

"None of your business, Miss, I'm sick of telling you I'm fine, will you explain this to me please," she angrily retorted pointing to her exercise book.

"Everything alright over there?" Mr. Price inquired, hearing the conversation between us.

"No problem, Florence is just frustrated with the exercise, we'll sort it out."

Florence became more agitated, possibly because of Mr. Price's inquiry; however, she slammed her book down, and ran out of the room. I wasn't sure if I should follow her out or not, but

Mr. Price indicated for me to stay in the classroom, and he left to find Florence.

He returned after five or ten minutes later, and continued as normal, teaching the class. He didn't remark to me, or the class, about the disturbance, either at that time or later. When the class had finished I approached him to ask if he had found Florence, his answer was,

"Girls of that age can be very temperamental and moody, especially at certain times of the month."

I thought this comment was unusual for a young male teacher to make, but then again I was 'old fashioned', and reserved about certain things which were talked about openly.

When I next saw June, I told her about the incident, and asked what she thought about Mr. Price. I needed her input from a parent's point of view.

"Well, my eldest one was in his class last year, before they went to Junior High, he thought he was great. He told me over and over again, that his teacher was 'one of us, from here, no airs and graces,' I got tired of hearing it. Why would a teacher want to be telling the kids he was from our part of the world, I know I wouldn't."

June shook her head despondently, and then continued.

"You know he told me the same thing, on the two occasions I had conversations with him, but I asked him why he came back, and he said that he just felt more comfortable with his own kind. Now as far as I am concerned, that is claptrap. I think our Mr. Price has something to hide, but then again my Freddie says I'm a cynical one."

I told June about my first impression of Mr. Price, and how I was impressed by his approach, but that recently my instincts were questioning his motivation.

"I think maybe we are looking too deep into Mr. Price's incentives, June, he's probably a fine, young teacher going back to his roots to give back to his community." I finally concluded.

I could see by June's reaction that she didn't agree with my last remark, however, we left the subject and enjoyed a nice fresh smoothie.

# Chapter 18
# Changing Direction.

I actually thought that my husband liked to see his business grow; however, he told me that James was getting a bit too big for his boots, and going alone on some decisions that should have been made by the Board of Directors. Also he was persuading Brad to do the same, and the upshot was that Brad disclosed these facts to my husband.

George was livid, and was calling an extra ordinary meeting of the Directors at his office. That evening he locked himself in his room to make copious notes and situations to point out, which he felt needed to be addressed at the meeting the next day.

He asked me not to disturb him, because he wanted, as Chairman, to call the shots. That evening he confided in me about this matter, which was very unusual. He would not normally disclose any discerning occurrences that were happening in his business. He did tell me that he learned a lot from the other partners; they had opened his horizons, and pushed him to take chances. They had expanded together into new fields of business, and increased their portfolios massively. Nevertheless, 'this was a company, and decision making could not to be independently made,' was how he described the problem to me.

"I think this is the fork in the road, Mary, "he announced as he went to the study.

The meeting, he told me had been scheduled for Saturday afternoon to allow for the partners to travel. Apparently, dependable Glenda had arranged the flights and the hotels, thankfully without their wives; I was not savoring the thought of a social evening with them.

I made a hearty breakfast for George, hoping this would confirm to him that I was behind him in his predicament, and wanted him to be strong in body as well as in mind. He was appreciative and humble with me that morning, maybe because he was in such a difficult position. He explained,

"I think it is the deceit I can't take, Mary. I opened the door of my established business, and welcomed James Turner in. Then he takes our company name, and our company money to support his office, for his own resources." He took large mouthfuls of his food before adding, "I know Brad is on my side, well, I hope he is."

He finished his breakfast and thanked me for being so dependable, and for being unquestionably open-minded. Again I was not sure if this was a positive or negative attribute for me to have, I never really thought of myself as an available protagonist, more as a 'stand by spouse,' which I thought he wanted me to be.

I waited anxiously for his return, imagining many scenarios that could result, and how this would, or could, affect my work at St John's. I was willing to be a supporting spouse as long as it didn't interfere with my newfound calling; perhaps George had not seen this trait in me?

It was around eight in the evening when he returned, heading straight for the drinks' cabinet, and consuming a large whisky. I didn't speak, but took his coat and kissed him on the cheek.

"I have a casserole slow cooking if you are hungry," I offered.

"Not just yet, maybe later. It's been a long arduous day with many open-ended decisions left on the table for tomorrow. Do you mind if I don't discuss it, Mary? I need to switch off, and maybe watch a little television."

"Sure, that's fine with me, George, I'll leave you to it, and I have things to do on my laptop."

I didn't pursue the matter further; he clearly was not ready to share anything with me that night.

I wanted to research Mr. Price on the internet. I knew I could find more about him on the school website that listed the staff, but I wanted to carry it further.

I discovered that John Price had a B.A. in Education from Drexel University, Sacramento, California. There was no mention of his birthplace. He had been at St John's for only two years. He was single and his interests were art and theater.

The next day George went to his office early, and came back after two hours.

"I didn't expect you to be back so quick." I remarked. "Is everything O.K.?"

I made a pot of coffee and we both sat at the kitchen table, for a long time in silence. Then he told me the startling news. It transpired that James Turner wanted to buy his way out of the company, and be in business on his own. Brad, who was the lawyer, drew up the papers overnight, and they were signed that day.

It seemed to suit Brad, who told George he felt happier when they were a small company, and that managing the New York office was a strain.

"You know, Mary, Brad is getting on in years, but I feel like I want to expand our business. It didn't work out with Turner, however, I must admit that I learned more from him than he did from me. I will definitely look into opening in Miami now we don't have the Washington office."

"Isn't that a little hasty, George?" I timidly asked. "Surely you need time to reconcile with your customers, and make sure James Turner hasn't whisked them away from you."

"How attentive of you, Mary, that was exactly Brad's opinion. I am too impatient, I want to expand, and expand we will. Life is passing us by; I need to set the ball rolling in that area, even if I don't open the office for the time being." He said in a crescendo.

I was relieved we were going to stay for a while, at least. I breathed a sigh of relief, and then I went over to kiss him. This comforting led him to believe I approved his plans, and so he continued,

"You know, Mary, I am glad James has left the company. This has given me the spurt I required. I can surge ahead now without all this accountability nonsense. I can handle Brad; James was not easy to manage. You might be seeing less and less of me for a while, dear, but I am sure you will understand."

"Yes. Dear." I smiled.

# Chapter 19
# Embarrassing Situations

Monday morning, and back in school, I learned I would be staying with Mr. Price's class for the time being. Barbara told me it was important for these children to have a good score at the end of term tests, before they went to Junior High. Apparently, it was essential for some of the children in that class to have extra help, so they could improve on their scores.

I reacted the same way to every one of my special needs children; I wanted Florence to feel at ease with me. In fact I was a little off hand, and asked her no personal questions, but stuck to the lesson problems for that day. She could tell by my reaction, I knew, but I didn't want to pry into her personal life anymore. If she asked, I would help, and I think she knew that.

Weeks went by in the usual routine way, but I couldn't help noticing when Florence stood up from her chair, and walked towards me she kept one hand on her stomach. A tell-tale signal that she was, in fact, pregnant.

She didn't look like she was putting on a lot of weight; in fact she looked very insipid and stressed out. I wanted to hug her, and comfort her, but I was there to give help in scholastic problems, not her personal ones.

I was trying to be objective; then again, I found myself watching Mr. Price's interaction with Florence, but in actual fact, he treated her just like the rest of the class. No more, no less attention was given to Florence in the classroom.

However, one afternoon I was walking towards my car when I saw them both together. Mr. Price, a tall man, was hugging Florence's petite frame, and whispering into her ear. She was definitely sobbing.

I was embarrassed, and uncomfortable looking at them both, I quickly got into my car and drove away in the opposite direction. I wanted to avoid them seeing me. I needed to leave quickly.

I didn't want to share with Barbara what I had seen, in case I was over thinking the situation. It could have been a teacher comforting an upset pupil, but Florence's accusation about Mr. Price blocked this thought from being reality. I kept the whole occurrence to myself.

The next day I asked Barbara, in a matter of fact way, what she thought about Mr. Price. She told me he was an ideal teacher for that grade, because male teachers in Elementary schools were hard to find, and the boys of that age were difficult to control. She liked the fact that he was an I.T. person.

The school couldn't afford many computers, but the few they did have were donations and needed upgrading, which Mr. Price carried out. She told me he also set up the room with the necessary connections.

She beamed as she said, "It would be wonderful to have laptops and wireless connections, but that wasn't in the budget for St John's." Then she continued keenly,

"Mr. Price also made our school's website, which saved us a lot of money, and he does spend many extra hours on the computers, researching and providing all of us who are not computer literate with the computer resources available on the net."

"I haven't seen the computers, where are they kept?, I asked.

She told me that Mr. Price had a large stock room, adjoining his classroom, which was a kind of mini lab.

"He is really the only one of us interested in using computers as a classroom tool, and his pupils are the relevant age to take advantage of them. So, it is appropriate for them to be there, but of course they are available for other teachers to use, if they so wish."

"I might want to use them sometime; do I need special permission from you or Mr. Price?" I queried.

"Heaven's sake, no, Mary, they are for every teacher to take advantage of. Anytime he is not using them, just use one."

During the break I quizzed Mr. Price on his prowess with computers.

"Did you major in that field during your University Studies? I read on your website that you went to Drexel in Sacramento." I added.

"No, I did Fine Arts and then a teaching diploma, but I have always been fascinated by the World Wide Web, as it is its gateway to so much information."

"Did you visit Sutter's Fort while you were studying there?"

He looked mystified at my query, but quickly told me he must get back to class.

"I haven't time to talk anymore, the children will be returning to class. We can chat another time. Come on, let's go."

I was curious why he didn't answer my question. Everyone knows that Sutter's Fort is perhaps the biggest tourist attraction in Sacramento. Was he ever in that capital city? Perhaps, again I was reading too much into a situation., and it was time I backed away. It wasn't important where, what, or why Mr. Price was evasive about his University life, he did know how to make a very good web page.

At the end of the school day I hung about in the classroom completing my reports. Everybody left, including Mr. Price. I located the stock room, switched on the light, and saw three, very old looking computers on tables.

I turned on the one farthest away from the door, and waited for it to show the screen saver. I had used computers all my adult life, so I was familiar with using this older model. I was not asked for a password to open it up, and the icons appeared on the desktop immediately. The icons were mostly recognizable; however, some were not.

Now I was sweating. I would not like to think someone would go into my computer, and then yet again this was not a personal computer, or was it? Barbara had told me I could use it. I was uneasy and nervous in case Mr. Price came in. I closed it down.

I walked towards the door, but then I turned back. I had a troubled thought, which I had to clear up. I switched on the other two computers, and was disturbed to discover that neither of them worked. I looked around the back of them and below, and they had no wiring or connections, apparently, they were not being used. Why had he only connected one computer?

My curiosity was getting the better of me, and I wanted to discover if it was being used as a personal computer or utilized as a teaching tool. I switched on the first computer once more. Instead of clicking the desktop icons, I went to the Google site, and used it as I would have done on my own laptop, searching recent sites visited. To my horror I pulled up several porn sites.

I was sickened. There were unbelievable images of young children, pictures of sex acts, and much more. I could no longer look. I returned to the desktop and opened one of the unfamiliar icons, which led me to similar sites. I closed everything down, left the room, and made for the bathroom. I was visibly shaking and felt nauseated right down to the pit of my stomach. I wished I hadn't pried about. I had opened a hornet's nest. I could never look into the eyes of Mr. Price again.

# Chapter 20
# Being The Good Wife

That evening I was happy to get back home and listen to my husband expound about his future plans. He told me there was a very important social evening taking place, which he wanted me to attend with him. He told me it was really significant to his advancement in business that we are noticeably seen together at this gathering. It was for a children's charity organization called 'Save the Children', so it was imperative he had me by his side.

I was willing to help this worthwhile charity; it was in my category of understanding, so I told him I would go.

"That's great. Mary. We don't have to dress too formal; it's not that kind of function. Casually smart, I think is fine. I will, of course, be giving a generous donation, but I need you to socialize with the right people. I will direct you to them, so no need to worry about that."

I pondered about the description of 'casually smart', and if I had such a thing in my wardrobe. My little black dress, I thought, would not fit into that category. I would check tomorrow; tonight I wanted to relax in the comfort of my own home with my husband. The dreadful images I had seen needed to be washed out of my mind. I would concentrate on making my husband happy.

The following morning I rang Barbara at the school, to say I had some personal commitments I needed to take care of, so I would not be able to go into school for at least a week. She understood, and reminded me once more that I was not an employee, but a volunteer, but she hoped I would support her again very soon.

I needed the time away from St John's, the information I had acquired from the school computer was something I had to digest, before I could fathom what to do with it.

I went to my wardrobe to see if I had anything that would be suitable for the function. I rummaged at the back where the clothes I use to dress in when I worked were hung. I pulled several out, and displayed them on the bed. I had various suits or many colors and types. I began trying them on, and was pleased to say they all fitted, so there was no need to shop, which is something I didn't want to do.

The evening of the function came, and I found myself happy to be going, along with my husband, to a gathering I wholeheartedly wanted to support. It started with a lot of speeches, about the work done that previous year, and then the lady behind the podium asked my husband to join her.

He went forward willingly, with a beaming smile, and a nod of his head, side to side as he acknowledged the crowd. She told the audience that my husband was their greatest benefactor, a pillar of society, and a wonderful supporter of their cause.

The audience applauded profusely, but I was uncertain why George didn't make it known who he was, or that it was his company money that had made the donation possible. I surmised that he just wanted to be recognized in the crowd later.

That was exactly his intention, as he subsequently told me. He was maneuvering his way into this social enclave for the ultimate motive of gaining them as future clients. My husband was getting very adept at marketing his persona, and I was not sure if I could uphold his principles as his spouse. I found it difficult to converse with some of the people. They asked me questions about George's business, I knew very little about so I quickly diverted the questioning to George, and made the excuse that I mainly spent my time doing voluntary work. This seemed to fit the bill admirably, and I made sure to move on around the room, so that they were not too inquisitive about where I did my volunteering.

On the way home, George praised me for my social skills, which I thought was over-rated; nevertheless, I was pleased I had played my part, and not embarrassed him in his quest for more business.

When we arrived home he wanted to celebrate the successful evening with a nightcap. I didn't refuse as I knew I could stay in bed the following day.  Over drinks, George once more brought up the subject of expanding his business to Florida, and then perhaps to the Islands or to South America.

I didn't respond to his escalating proposals, I had no wish to suppress his enthusiasm for the business getting bigger. He was in his own world, and content to voice his thoughts out loud to a willing listener.

Thankfully, he did admit that this process would take a lot of planning and research to trade in foreign countries, and maybe he would have to travel there to explore the possibilities before taking the plunge and opening down there.

I agreed with him, and then he asked if I would like to go with him. I hastily replied that I would be more of a hindrance to him, and he would do better asking Brad or someone from the office who would be more able to share in his inquiries.

"Well. If you don't mind me being absent for stretches of time, I will make other arrangements. I am just so pleased you are being so supportive, Mary. Don't worry about money while I am away, I'll make sure you have money in our joint account you can draw from."

I was satisfied I had managed to escape the travelling, without appearing to be uncooperative. Regarding his offer of leaving me more money in our account, I knew I wouldn't need it. I spent very little on myself; my expenses were for gas and food. Occasionally I went to the thrift shop to buy clothes or books for St John's, but that was a very small amount.

That thought reminded me that I eventually had to face Mr. Price again. I wasn't going to make accusations against him too soon; I had to have more concrete proof that he was unsuitable for his post at St. John's, before I went that far.

The next day I called Barbara to tell her I would be in school the following Monday. She seemed pleased that I was returning, and thanked me again for being such a reliable volunteer.

Since I had a few more days at home, I decided to see what I could find out about Mr. John Price. I put in his name on a Google search, and hoped something would appear. At first several people with the same name came up, both the first and last names were very common. They all seemed to have a Facebook account, which I would have to explore. This was time consuming, but at last I had more information to go on.

# Chapter 21
# Facing the Inevitable

I nervously went into school, not understanding why I should feel that way, but I was uncertain if Mr. Price did know I had been using 'his' computer.

Thankfully, everything seemed to be normal. He greeted me enthusiastically, telling me I had been sorely missed by both him and the pupils. He held out his hand which I uneasily shook.

Barbara, along with some of the staff, informed me they had read an article about the charity event. They wondered if it was me, and my husband who were mentioned in the article. I had to reluctantly tell them it was, but I quickly changed the subject to avoid more questioning.

Back in Mr. Price's classroom, I was asked to continue with the extra tutoring I gave to the special needs children, who, of course, included Florence. I observed her appearance and demeanor, but there seemed to be no bulge showing. She just looked very tired and weary, which affected me a great deal. I just wanted to wrap my arms around her, and reassure her that I would be there for her, if needed. However, I knew in my heart I could not do this openly, the same as I had witnessed John Price doing.

At the break I cautiously asked Mr. Price if there was a school computer I could use. I mentioned that the Principal had informed me they had some donated. He answered quickly,

"Yes we did have some donated, but I am still working on them. They are very old, and I am trying to fix them on a shoestring budget. I'll let you know when they are ready to use."

"Great! In the meantime I will bring in my own lap top to use when I need it." I quickly responded. "I just thought I could write my reports down more speedily and neatly on a computer."

"Oh, I agree Ms. Daniels. You know I obtained my degree online. It was hassle free, and far more convenient."

I congratulated him before excusing myself to go to the staff room. I didn't want to give the impression I was too inquisitive about his circumstances.

It was a few days later when I again saw Florence in a comparable situation. She was walking hand in hand with a young boy I did not recognize. I was sure he didn't attend St John's because he looked to be much older, maybe a High School pupil?

I was in my car driving home, but I parked and kept them in sight. They turned into another street, so I followed slowly, and then I parked once more because they had stopped to join a group of youths standing on the corner.

They seemed to know Florence's companion, and were laughing and gesturing towards them. I wondered if they knew Florence's condition, and were perhaps mocking and making sarcastic remarks to her. I wanted to jump out of the car to her defense, although I knew that would be more embarrassing for her.

I decided to confront her the next day, and ask if she had a boyfriend, which I did, and she answered,

"I don't think that is any of your business, Miss, but if you really want to know. I do have a one." Then she poked her nose up in the air brazenly, and walked away.

I was left feeling self-conscious about the encounter. She was right, I was wrong to ask such a personal question. I decided once more to focus my attention on the real reason I was at St John's, which was to assist in the classrooms, and not interfere into the private lives of the staff or pupils.

I tried to be more resolute in my decision, which lasted only a few days. I couldn't help noticing that at the end of the school day, when I was clearing away the textbooks, Mr. Price disappeared into the store room. His excuse was, that he was working on the computers, trying to get them functioning so they could be used. I just pictured in my head the icons on the working computer, I only responded with a simple salutation,

"See you tomorrow, have a good evening." I said biting my tongue. He certainly would have an enjoyable evening in his way!

On the drive home I mulled in my head the two possibilities regarding Florence's pregnancy. I considered what she had told June, that the Father was Mr. Price. He definitely was a sneaky character with a promiscuous obsession. I also had seen him embracing Florence, and whispering in her ear. On the other hand she did have a boy friend, who didn't mind showing her off to his street cronies.

Once more I tried to wipe the images out of my head, and concentrate on driving home safely.

That evening when I reached home, June was still there. George had asked her to do some spring cleaning, and she didn't mind at all as she could always use the extra money. I made a pot of coffee, and suggested she join me when her task was finished. I was curious to know more about Florence's family.

June had not known the family very long, apparently they had just moved to Lower Bridgewater a few years ago. She did recognize that the wife knew very little about birth control, as her large brood was obviously born with scarcely a year apart of each other. She went on to tell me that they seemed to be a very close-knit family. The older ones took care of the younger ones, to give their Mother a break.

"I have noticed as well that Florence is very close to her brother. In fact if you saw them out together you would think they were girlfriend and boyfriend, not a brother and sister. He protects her from the bad lot he knocks around with, it's no surprise they are so close. My husband tells me that her brother vetoes who she can go around with, but I suppose that's not a bad thing around our neighborhood." June sighed as she finished, and sipped her coffee.

She then asked me if I knew anything more about Florence's pregnancy, and her accusation about Mr. Price. I told her I had seen Florence hand in hand with a boy, and also about Mr. Price embracing her, but I did leave out what I discovered on his computer.

June questioned me about the boy, what he looked like, and how old he appeared. However, I did not see him close up, so all I could say was that he looked to be older than Florence.

"I asked Florence outright did she have a boyfriend, and she told me that she did have one, but it was none of my business."

June smiled and supported Florence's remark, but then she added that all we knew for certain was that Florence was pregnant, though we had no idea who the Father was.

"I do feel sorry for the Mother, she has enough children to look after now without adding another to the family. Her husband drinks heavily, and her children run wild.  I think she has given up trying to keep them under control, the poor woman's a wreck."

# Chapter 22
# Pushing Ahead in Business

When George arrived home from work he told me about asking June to do some extra cleaning.

"I think I am ready to expand into Florida, Mary, things are looking pretty good down there. We ought to test the real estate market here, to see what kind of price we might get, and whether our kind of property is changing hands." He paused only a few minutes before adding,

"I don't want to put it in a realtor's hands just yet. Maybe you could do some research yourself first, so we could get an idea of prices. After all, that was the business you were in before you were pregnant."

There he was again, reaching a decision even before I had a chance to comment. Fortunately, I had my back to him, setting the table for dinner, and he failed to see the shock and anxiety on my face. Even so, he carried on with his plans; diplomacy was not George's strong point.

He told me about his many visits to Florida, which he had taken with his trustworthy secretary, Glenda. They had made contacts down there from recommendations and referrals given to him by his existing clients, additionally these had been invaluable engagements that produced even more customers.

"You know, dear, we haven't even started to look into the markets in the Islands; Antigua, Trinidad, Turks and Cacaos, St John. Oh, the possibilities are endless!" he exclaimed rubbing his hands together.

Thank goodness he wasn't expecting a comment from me; I was bewildered, and rather taken aback by his sudden revelations. It wasn't as if his expansion plans were new to me. They had always been on the cards since James Turner had left the company; however, I think I had put them at the back of my mind, and now I had to accept they were a probability, and not a possibility.

His tenacious mind-set about moving to Florida was proving to be an imminent event. He had already seen two potential offices, situated in prime locations in downtown Miami. He had also seen an apartment to rent on a short-term basis that was convenient to get to these offices without needing to drive; apparently, he could use a metrorail service.

"Of course, dear, I don't expect you to live in the apartment, or ride the metro. We will buy a house in a good area, in the outskirts, and of course get you a better car," he said, still not looking at me or seeking my opinion on the choice.

"But I don't know anyone in Miami, George. I have heard it is a very large Hispanic area, and I don't speak Spanish."

"We both have to make adjustments, just as we did when we moved here. Now don't be negative about this development, it's for a better future, Mary. Together we can raise our standard of living to heights we never dreamed of when we first met."

He had the bit between his teeth, and was racing forward with his ideas. George insisted I would make friends easily once he had established the right circles to be in down there. He attempted to charm me with flattery, expounding his belief in my intellect and poise. There was no turning back for him; nothing was going to stand in his way. I was being drawn into a new life, in a new city, with no alternative.

I could not use my volunteering work at St John's as an excuse to stay, since it was an unpaid position. The pleasure and fulfillment I got from doing it would be lost on George. He equated work with money, and his satisfaction came from making more money. We had no family ties to keep us from moving, no economic restrictions. I could not fathom any conceivable reason to stay, that would be a viable excuse. Perhaps our house would be hard to sell, and I could stay behind until it sold, was one of my positive thoughts just then. However, I knew that was unreal, and would never happen.

    I did look at websites on my laptop that advertised houses for sale in our area, and saw the values. To my dismay, they were fetching very good prices, as the sites indicated it was "a very desirable area", so they were selling fast. I was reluctant to immediately give George this information. The longer I could stall him, the better it was for me. Fortunately, he was so absorbed in his business development plans; he consequently didn't follow up on my research right away.

    During the next few weeks George went on many trips to Florida. He had rented an apartment, and was working from it. Apparently, he found it very convenient to start his preliminary groundwork from there.

"I do need to employ a good secretary, Mary, and I hope Brad can recommend a good corporate lawyer. They both are essential to me before I can move forward,"

"What about Glenda? Does she not want to move to a warmer climate?" I suggested.

"Well, I haven't proposed anything to her at the present time because she is so essential to our office here, but it has crossed my mind. She is utterly reliable, and knows the business so well," he hastily answered.

He also told me he was thinking of closing the office, and moving the company completely to headquarters in Miami. He indicated that Brad could have the clients in the North, and he would take care of the Southern States and the Caribbean.

"Does Brad know about this proposal of yours?" I asked.

"I haven't run this past him yet, it's only an idea at the present time. I have no doubt I can persuade him though, Brad is a very plausible guy, and pretty much goes along with all my suggestions."

I didn't respond to his last remark, as I considered his proposal would add time, to my plan, of delaying the move to Florida for as long as possible. George was meticulous when it came to preparation, so I just encouraged him to do what was best for his business.

I was relieved and thankful he was going to be too busy in the coming months, to impede my volunteering work at St John's.

# Chapter 23
# The Unexpected

I was enjoying my volunteering work, and basically I felt I was doing something meaningful and useful. Barbara never hesitated to thank me for being there; she actually told me that I was invaluable to the staff and to the pupils. This encouragement spurred my motivation to do my very best while I was there.

Instead of researching real estate on my laptop, I would look for word games or puzzles that would support my teaching to the special needs children. I wanted them to enjoy learning, and not feel it was a burden. In most cases it worked, some of the children even asked for more 'games' to play.

During the lunch period I let some of them use my laptop to share programs that would encourage them to work together, and solve problems. Of course, I was there to supervise, and didn't mind eating my sandwich with them in the classroom.

This prompted me to ask Mr. Price if he had made progress fixing the computers, so the pupils could have more access to the internet.

Predictably, he had excuses, of being because of the cost-cutting measures, or a time factor, or simply he was working on them. I let the matter go over my head, and didn't pursue my inquiries further.

I was disappointed I couldn't get Florence to participate in these sessions. She informed me that she preferred to eat lunch with her brother and not her classmates. One pupil described her as "a mixed up bitch" whom I quickly admonished that his choice of words was not courteous in polite company. He acknowledged that he didn't know any other way to describe her, so I accepted his apology.

It was clear Florence was not liked by her peers, and this probably explained why she spent more time with her brother. The only other person, who accepted and gave her consideration, seemed to be her teacher Mr. Price. She was a vulnerable child looking for love and attention, wanting to be liked, but uneasy when it was in unfamiliar situations. I felt she was putting on this austere bravado when I spoke to her, to conceal her unsure reasoning. Florence did not trust my intentions were anything but sincere. I was in unfamiliar territory, and I couldn't find a way to make her feel at ease with me.

One Monday morning I came into the classroom to find the children huddled together in groups, whispering and noisily making gestures that definitely were not appropriate. I got their attention, and asked them to line up ready to go to assembly. Mr. Price came into the room, rather annoyed, and in a disgruntled fashion, told the class to proceed to the assembly.

I was following, but Barbara stopped me in the corridor to give me some bad news. Florence's Father had committed suicide over the weekend, and in this close-knit society everyone seemed to be familiar with the news. She didn't know when or how he had done this, but she didn't think that Florence would be in school.

I was at a loss for words, and didn't know how to react to the information.

"What is the appropriate response in these circumstances?" I asked tentatively.

Barbara was unsure, but she did say it was a delicate situation, and maybe we should wait until the school was formally notified by the authorities.
All sorts of scenarios were being passed around by the pupils and the staff; however, Mr. Price's demeanor was nonchalant. He continued

his teaching schedule with no reactions to the ongoing gossip.

I was troubled about the consequences his passing would have on that large family, and worried, concerned that there would be yet another mouth to feed very soon. I couldn't keep this anxious feeling to myself much longer, and I really had to share my concerns with the Principal.

I decided to have this conversation with Barbara, as a friend and not as a member of staff. I left it to the end of the school day, and decisively made my approach to her office. I passed by her secretary and in a polite, but superior voice told her I had some Alumni news for the Principal. Barbara met me with a smile, however she detected I was not there for a simple chit-chat.

"You look awful, Mary, please sit down, and tell me what is troubling you," she said in a truly sympathetic voice.

I didn't know where to begin, and I was unaware how much she really knew about the condition of Florence. I decided to come forward with this basic information, and then expand from there.

"Barbara, did you know that Florence was pregnant?"

Her chin dropped and her eyes stared at me. She opened her mouth, but nothing came out. She shook her head side to side to verify her obvious ignorance of Florence's predicament. Then she whispered,

"Mary, she is too young, who would do this to an innocent child?"

I went on to explain my various speculations. I told her that Florence had indicated Mr. Price was the Father, but Barbara answered again by shaking her head without saying anything. I put her into the picture of the young boy I saw Florence with, and how close they seemed to be.

"I asked Florence if she had a boyfriend, and she reluctantly told me she had, but it was none of my business."

This little bit of information brought a slight smile to Barbara's face, however it didn't last long, and she thoughtfully replied.

"We can't change the fact that Florence could be pregnant, and because of her age, I have to report this supposition to the right authority, for them to determine the correct procedure."

It was my turn to nod my head instead of replying. I was uncertain about adding my findings about a member of staff to this scenario. Mr. Price was definitely in the equation, but his devious activities online added another perspective to this matter. I put my elbows on the desk, and my hands, for a second, covered my face. I dropped the fingers of both my hands over by mouth, and looked sternly into Barbara's distressed eyes.

"Is there more?" she asked anxiously.

I nodded again, and then I sat back in my chair to give her a full account of everything I had found out, and seen regarding her teacher, Mr. Price. I ended with the scene I witnessed of Mr. Price comforting Florence as he whispered in her ear.

A long silence followed between us. I could see she was trying to relate to this situation as two friends would do, and also deciding as a school principal what her duties were. I tried to relieve some of the tension.

"Barbara, you know I would only be truthful with you. I have no animosity against Mr. Price. I think his abilities as a teacher are unquestionable, but the material on his computer was there, and was easily accessible. Maybe if we went there now, you could see for yourself, and verify my findings?"

"We will do just that," she curtly answered.

We walked together through an empty secretary's office and into the corridor where the janitor was working with his staff. I hadn't realized we had been talking so long, and the school was empty of staff and pupils.

The janitor greeted the Principal and me in a courteous manner, and then continued working. As we walked in silence towards the classroom I suddenly had a panic feeling. What if he had erased all the evidence of his pursuits? I would be left in a terrible situation. I was even dreading the fact that he could be there in the stockroom, and if so what could be the outcome.

We walked into an empty classroom with only the evening sunlight guiding our way. Barbara gestured with her finger over her mouth and her arm on mine, to stand still, and listen. We recognized then that someone was in the stock room. Sniggering sounds came from the room, followed by gleeful exclamations of ecstasy. I looked at Barbara, who had nausea written all over her face, and I knew that feeling from my first encounter with Mr. Price's unhealthy addiction.

Quietly Barbara turned the doorknob, and we entered the dark windowless room. The light of the computer displayed directly towards us revealing the truth of my testimony, he was encroached in child pornography. In fact he was so enchanted with the display on the screen that he was oblivious of our presence.

"Excuse me, Mr. Price," Barbara shouted, "exactly what are you up to on my school premises?"

She didn't stop with her tirade of expletives giving him no chance to answer, or explain his predicament. Walking towards him slowly, but deliberately, he had no time to move from his seat. He stared back at her. I really thought she was going to slap his face, but instead she poked him with her finger and said,

"I trusted you with our pupils, you pervert, leave now before I get the police here to lock you away. I never want to see your depraved face again. You wicked, immoral man, get out of my sight!"

I was uneasy as to how Mr. Price would react to Barbara's abuse; fortunately he didn't say a word, but stood and walked slowly towards me. I moved side-wards to let him through the door; however, he menacingly looked directly into my face, with disdain.

"This is your doing, you toffee-nosed interfering bitch. The children in MY class never liked you around. Everything was fine until you came here, and you're not even qualified to be instructing in a classroom. I AM."

He shouted the last two words as he exited the room, and hastily passed through his classroom without a second glance. I turned to see Barbara sitting on his chair with her back to the computer. Tears were running down her cheeks, but her hands were clasped together on her knees, and she was shaking.

I put my arms around her ample body to comfort her. I told her softly and gently that we should go to her office, and get away from this detrimental situation.

"Let's get back to sanity, you'll feel better in your own room to make you next decision. Come on, I'll see if I can muster up a hot drink for us."

"Switch that thing off, Mary, if you will, and ask the janitor to lock this stock room. I have to make an urgent phone call."

# Chapter 24
# Finding answers

George had made great strides in his business matters and, as expected, Brad had agreed to everything my husband wanted to happen. The head office was going to be relocated to Miami, with reliable secretary Glenda willing to join the staff there. He had also interviewed and hired additional personnel who were bilingual, and able to deal with his expansion schemes.

"I have taken a lease on the downtown offices I was interested in, so my dear, we are ready for our house hunt. Have you researched any areas you might want to live in? I think that should be a priority before we hire a realtor in Miami."

There he was again with the proverbial 'we'; however, it was more important that I slow him down with the house hunt.

"George, first things first, I have been working at selling our house here," then I added untruthfully, "but I have been advertising it on the web 'By Owner' so if you want to speed things up we will have to get a realtor to do it for us."

With baited breath, I waited for his answer.

"I will have to leave these matters for you to deal with. Whatever you decide, Mary, is fine by me. Just make it happen very soon; I need you to be by my side when I attend these social functions. I have been really surprised at how many there are to attend in Miami. You will love the balmy sunsets, and the warm sea breezes. Many of these social events take place in beautiful settings, so a new wardrobe for you is yet another task for you to complete, dear."

Only the eating of his dinner silenced George from his descriptions of life in Miami. He was in euphoria explaining to me the various locations that were possible for us to live, and eventually he came to the conclusion that he would look for potential houses in Miami, and I could concentrate on getting our present house sold.

I felt like I was on a roller coaster ride to Miami with no stops in sight. I had been given my agenda to comply with what seemed simple enough to George, but was filled with dread for me. Even so, I had to abide by his request. My husband's business was moving to Miami, no, had moved to Miami, and I did not have a choice, but to support him.

I signed a contract with a realtor the following day, and left it for fate to decide my destiny.

I tried to combat my negative thoughts by comparing my situation to poor Florence's. I told myself to be grateful for my circumstances, and positively look ahead to new horizons.

I went into St John's that day with a new vigor. My time had been cut short for making tangible changes, but I wanted to try. I made my way to Barbara's office to find out her strategy for dealing with Mr. Price and his class.

Her secretary welcomed me with a detached 'good morning' as I went through to the Principal. Barbara was filling in paperwork, but indicated I should sit down. Finally, she looked up at me. She had a dejected and sad expression, as she spoke.

"I've had very little sleep in the last few days, Mary. I wanted desperately to keep this matter away from bad publicity for the school's sake. I finally put the matter before the governors to let them decide what to do about Mr. Price. They have been very supportive, and have taken over the formal procedures; however, I have had to write numerous reports for them, and for the police. Above everything, I don't want this leaking out to the press. So far so good."

She had decided to bring in a substitute for Mr. Price and tell the pupils he was off sick. The abhorrent computer had been seized by the police, obviously to back up the accusations made by Barbara, and the governors.

"I'm afraid they also want you to write a statement about your involvement with Mr. Price. Are you willing to do this, Mary?"

"Of course," I replied, "anything to help."

I wondered where she would like to place me that day, adding before she answered I would be best placed, for continuity sake, in Mr. Price's class with the substitute teacher. She agreed, and I left her to finish the endless paperwork that had to be done.

The substitute was a young man with an athletic body. Unknown to me, but a familiar face to the boys in the class. Apparently, he had played basketball for a famous college team, and therefore his face had been seen many times on television. The class's welcome to this new face overcame any questioning about Mr. Price's absence. The boys were ecstatic to have such a celebrated player as their teacher, and the girls were transfixed by his physical appearance.

This choice of substitute by Barbara was ideal; it took the limelight away from petty speculations about Mr. Price's absence, as well as the topic of Florence and her family. This class had boasting rights to expound about. Their morale was high, and fortunately his demand for their attention needed little persuasion. He had them eating out of his hands before the morning was over. His new fresh approach was satisfying the pupils' previous lethargic attitudes to learning. He was, in fact, a tangible role model for St John's, just at the right time.

Florence did not appear in school, and I couldn't help wondering how she and her family were coping with their loss. I didn't want to interfere, however, I was certain Florence would be showing her pregnancy, and therefore would not want outside authorities prying into her condition. I went to Barbara to get some direction, and acknowledgment as to the correct procedure to take with this matter.

She admitted it was a dilemma for her. She should respond, as a Principal, to the parents for not sending their child to school, and ask for an explanation because they were breaking the law. On the other hand, she was acquainted with the circumstances, and she did not want to open a

Pandora's Box for the Mother with whom she sympathized with.

"Would it be appropriate for me, as your representative, to go to the house to try to evoke a response, and give our condolences about their loss?" I cautiously asked.

Barbara sat silently pondering my suggestion, and its feasibility; however, she shook her head in bewilderment. This was a situation she had never encountered before, and the challenge of doing the right thing on a professional level as well as a personal one was draining her impulses.

For the next half hour we toyed with the various scenarios, and the possible repercussions. Mutually we realized the seriousness of an underage child being pregnant, by an unknown person, and the double whammy of a Father who had committed suicide. Both situations were really hypothetical, as we had no real proof, only hearsay to validate our assertions. It was a delicate situation that would take a gentle approach to deal with.

Finally we agreed that if I went to the home it should be in the auspices of conveying the school's condolences for the family's loss. Perhaps taking a basket of food along with a card should be the appropriate stance, which would enable me to learn the conditions in the home, and where, if anywhere we could help further, was Barbara's conclusion.

I was happy we had talked our way through the quandary and reached a sensible approach. We were like-minded people, and equally intelligent to know the consequences of rushing into situations we were not familiar with. I would take care of everything, and promised Barbara I would be very discrete, making the visit look like a normal response from the children's' school. I would only refer to the Father's passing, and not to the circumstances we couldn't confirm.

I carefully chose the card to be non-religious, and simply wrote inside the card 'From the Staff of St John's'. I found a basket I had stored in my garage, and then I asked June what she thought were basic food items to put in a needy person's pantry, without disclosing who the recipient was.

She wrote me a list, but then added that it was possible to give a gift token from most grocery stores rather than fill a basket, and then the person could decide what to spend the money on. This was a very sensible approach, but I knew Florence's Mother would be tied in the home with her younger children, and I really didn't trust the older ones to shop for essentials.

Barbara had given me $100 to spend, so I decided to fill the basket with some of the items on the list, and put the remainder of money inside the card. I did the shopping with great care, and placed the items into the basket on top of some face cloths, then covered them with several new tea towels I had in my store at home. This way the basket didn't look too opulent for the Mother to receive.

I decided to visit the home during school hours because I envisage the older children, with the exception of Florence, would be in school. I carefully put the basket with the card in my trunk, and headed for Lower Bridgewater.

I didn't park in front of the house, but in the side street. There were very few people around, so my short walk with my basket to the door was not conspicuous. I knocked, and waited until I heard someone shout.

"Answer the dam well door wil' yer, I've got mi hands full ye numb skull, a clout around yer ears is what you deserve to get yer moving."

I stared at the shoddy front door as I waited, noticing the paint peeling off, and the broken tiles on the step. It was, however, a solid wooden door that squeaked, as it hung on to the one hinge. It slowly opened to reveal the startled face of Florence, and her very pregnant body. I spoke gently and quietly telling her I had brought a gift for her family from the Principal and staff, as a token of our sympathy at the loss of her Father.

"Who the hell are yer talking to Florrie, for God's sake girl, if it aint the police then let im in."

Florence cautiously opened the door wider for me to get through, but quickly she pushed passed me, to explain whom I was, and why I was there. I expected to see her Mother feeding or attending to a young child, but instead I saw an unkempt, hefty woman sitting in filth with one hand holding a beer can, and the other holding a cigarette.

The smell in the room was nauseous, and I found it hard to open my mouth, and put into words why I was there. Fortunately, Florence did the explaining for me, taking the basket from my hands and putting it on the sofa next to her Mother.

She put the can down on the sofa undeterred by the spillage, and left the cigarette hanging out of the side of her mouth as she rummaged in the basket.

"There is a card there to express our condolences, we are sorry for your loss. The Principal and the staff of St John's all send their sympathies."

I remained standing in front of her as she emptied the contents on to the sofa next to her. I could swear she was sniggering, but it may have been her inhaling the cigarette without taking it out of her mouth. I watched as she inspected each item until she came to the card.

"Here, read that for us Florrie, I can't seem to focus in this light," she demanded passing the card to her daughter.

Florence curiously opened the envelope, and looked inside. I could see by her reaction she had seen the notes as well as the card, however, she managed to pull out the card leaving the money inside. Her Mother was still scrutinizing the cans and packets as Florence read out loud the salutation in the card. I noticed she put the envelope discreetly into her pocket before passing the card to her Mother, who grabbed it. Then despite the consequence, put it down on top of the spilled can of beer at her side.

I could hear children playing together in the next room, obviously unsupervised, by their unconcerned Mother. I wanted to escape from this hell-hole that Florence lived in, yet I felt guilty leaving her there to cope with the state of affairs that existed,

"Get mi another beer and make yourself useful girl," griped the distasteful woman.

Florence was obviously hardened to this occurrence and went to the kitchen to get her Mother another beer. In the meantime, I made my excuses to leave. This unfit Mother continued to chain smoke, putting down the butt into the overflowing ashtray, and lighting up another cigarette.

I indicated to Florence to follow me to the door, and once there I asked her if she would walk with me to my car, using the excuse that I was not quite sure if I had left it in a safe place.

We walked in silence, but as I reached my car Florence started to apologize for her Mother's behavior, and the condition of the house.
"But that is not your fault, Florence. It is your Mother's job to look after her children, and especially you in your condition." I said, without expecting the reaction my words would have.

Florence began to sob uncontrollably so I opened the passenger door and gently, but firmly, asked her to sit inside to calm down. I opened the driver's door, and sat quietly beside her. I offered her a packet of tissues, which I had in the glove compartment, and watched with concern as she gave a cathartic release to her pent up anxiety.

## Chapter 25
## If truth were known.

Steadily, Florence's weeping lessened, and turned into silent tears that still flowed down her cheeks. I was reluctant to touch her, even though I was tempted to do so. She seemed to be rigidly sitting upright in the seat, her body language not giving way to her inner emotions.

She wiped her tears, and composed herself. Then she began to speak, intermittently, between wiping her face to soak up the flow that endlessly streamed from her eyes. She was breathing heavily, gasping for air, but still holding herself stiffly, as though her words were meant to be heard clearly, and not muffled by the tissue.

Florence held her head high, willing the tears to stay within. Her hands were clasped tightly together on her knees.

"My Mother is a bully, ......to us all, Miss. She uses her cursing, and her fists to get her own way. All she is interested in is getting a good supply of her beer and cigarettes."

I wanted to console her, I wanted to hug her, but I realized she hadn't finished, so I gulped my words back, and instead, turned my body towards her. Florence didn't look back at me, but stared through the windscreen, obviously, waiting for my reaction. When it didn't come, she continued.

"All us kids look after each other, we have to. It's hard to find money for food, that's why I didn't give her the money in the envelope; she would have spent it on booze. My older brothers manage to get money, but I don't ask where from, we have to feed the young 'uns."

There was a lull in her confessions, so I proffered a tentative question.

"Why didn't your Father help?"

She didn't answer straight away, and in the silence I wondered if he committed suicide to escape from his responsibilities.

"You might not believe me, Miss, but she bullied him also. I mean big-time. She would punch him with her fists, wallop him with her beer cans, and hit him with what ever was lying around. The screeching and yelling would frighten the babies, but that didn't deter her."

She paused for a second before adding. "Who would believe that a man can be beaten up by his wife? Even my brothers were no match for her after a drinking binge."

After taking in a few heavy deep breaths, she continued.

"Recently, she's been mixing the booze with the hard stuff. God knows where she got that from, but the result was crazy, she was wicked, especially towards mi Dad."

At this point I did take her hands into mine, and squeezed them gently. Florence went on to tell me that she tried to comfort her Dad, after the fights, but he was devastated. In the stillness of the moment, I wondered if Florence's Father was too overwhelmed with his situation, too ashamed to bring in the authorities, so he ended his life. I kept my thoughts to myself.

As though she was reading my thoughts, Florence gave incredible justification to the situation.

"Mi Dad just wanted loving. He could cry on my shoulder, and tell me how he hated everything that was going on. I listened, Miss, I cared about him. He couldn't go to anybody else. He is ….was a good man. He did his best, Miss, but he was no match for mi Mother."

Florence was not crying anymore. She began to rationalize with a determined voice, her love for her father. I told her, with the same unwavering support, that she was a good girl for caring about her Father, and it was a fine thing to do under the circumstances.

Nonetheless, she shook her head as her eyes dropped to the floor of the car. Then she looked up, and her eyes met mine.

"Yes Miss, but I tried too hard; I didn't think he would do that. He shouldn't have left me." She bawled as her tears returned.

At this point I had to give her comfort. I wrapped my arms around her, carefully trying to give her swollen belly room between us.

"It wasn't your fault, Florence. Your Father made his own choice, and you couldn't have anticipated that happening, don't blame yourself." I said patting her shoulder.

She pushed me away, and with a tight smile replied. "But it was, I asked for it. I wanted it to go further, I encouraged him. We did it a lot, I did it to spite my Mother, she didn't want him, and she didn't love him. I did."

I tried to make sense of what she was saying, and I looked at her quizzically, waiting for confirmation.

With malice mixed with fear she replied angrily, patting her stomach, "Yes this is the result, and I have no regrets."

I was stunned, but I tried hard to hide my utter shock at her revelation. Florence sat straight-backed, stiff, defiantly looking towards me for my reaction. I gulped a few times and moistened my dry lips before speaking.

"Did you know you were doing wrong, Florence? Did you Father make you do it?"

"No he did not," she quickly replied, "I was the one; it was me who encouraged him. I cared for him, mi Mother didn't."

After this outburst, Florence opened the car door, and ran hastily down the street towards her house. She acted so quickly, I didn't foresee her leaving our talk, and I knew it was pointless following her. As a result, I sat dazed, watching her disappear back to her tormented existence.

Finally, I pulled myself together, walked around and closed the passenger door before driving away from Lower Bridgewater. My mind was reeling from Florence's revelation; it was hard for me to concentrate on driving, however I needed to get back to the sanctuary of my own home, so I did my best to concentrate on the road ahead, and not dwell on situations I couldn't change.

# Chapter 26
# Moving On

I reached home relieved to find it empty. George was in Florida, and June had left. My head was reeling with information I couldn't assimilate. I felt physically sick. As I filled the kettle with water, my hands were shaking so much that it was difficult for me to accomplish this simple task. I put it on the stove, and sat at the kitchen table contemplating what I should do about Florence's disclosure. She was a vulnerable child whose own Father had used her, and then left her to face the consequences. Why did she have to tell me?

The whistling of the kettle brought me back to the present moment, carefully I made an instant coffee for myself, routinely carrying out the process to block out all other thoughts. I placed the mug on the table with unsteady hands, and recognized at that moment I had been put in a situation I was unable to handle.

I had to share this dilemma with the only possible person who could do the right thing about it. I was far more concerned about the result for Florence than I had been about Mr. Price, but nevertheless, Barbara was the one person who would treat this delicate problem with the care it needed.

I finished my coffee before making the call, all the time wondering if I should make known the true facts about Florence. I had been her confidant, her sounding board; could I disclose her to the community? Would the outcome be something she could cope with? Her Father definitely could not take the consequences; the cost was left on the shoulders of a small child who only wanted to be loved.

I carefully related to Barbara the events that took place, cautiously telling her the situation in Florence's home, so she might fully understand the final end result. I explained the Mother's condition, the concealing of money, and the hopeless predicament Florence was in, before I revealed the ultimate, crucial fact.

There was a gasp from the other end, and then silence. The significance of the matter had obviously affected Barbara, as it did me, and we were both equally stunned. I started to defend Florence in an effort to stimulate the conversation back to reality, but I needn't have tried, because Barbara completely agreed with me. This was not a Mr. Price scenario; Florence was too naïve to realize the outcome of her actions. Mr. Price deserved to be punished.

We talked at length about possible solutions, and ultimately we agreed that it had to be a social welfare matter, and they had to protect Florence from her dysfunctional Mother. I agreed wholeheartedly with Barbara so once more this reliable friend and Principal, took on the undertaking of a fragile problem at St John's. I was happy to relinquish the obligation to her capable hands.

Before hanging up, Barbara made one more suggestion.

"I think you should take a break from us for a little while, Mary. You deserve to put back a bit of normality back into your life."

I certainly needed to hear her proposal; it released me from feeling guilty about my inept ability to deal with the day-to-day occurrences in Little Bridgewater. I needed a new, fresh task that was on my doorstep, and I knew just what that was. I made a call to the realtor to push for a sale of our property, even if we had to drop the price.

For the first time in months I was eager to see George, and listen to his enthusiastic stories about Miami. I wanted to hear some inspiring, exciting information, instead of the corrupting, debasing matters I had been challenged with. I called George on his cell, hoping it wouldn't go to his voice box.

It rang a few times, but then he answered. I tried to sound perky and unemotional, not wanting him to realize how depressed I was.

"Hi George, how are things going down there? I just wanted to know if you would agree to lower our house price, if it became necessary."

"Well, I will be home on Friday, so maybe we can discuss our options then, if that suits?" He answered pleasantly, but then with more gusto he added, "I have a lot of great news for you, Mary, I think a celebration dinner is in order, will you book us a table at the Italian place you like?"

"Of course George, I'll look forward to it. See you Friday. Take care."

As I put the receiver down I became conscious of the fact I was ready to be spoiled by my husband. I wanted to be pampered and loved. I was no different than Florence and her Father on that score. It was a basic animal instinct, a natural feeling, if the circumstances were right.

I didn't want to become morbid again, so I quickly put that thought out of the way, and opened my laptop to search the property websites.

Then, as though our realtor was reading my mind she called to ask if she could arrange an 'open house' for our property on Sunday.

"Of course, that sounds splendid." I replied, "Do we have to leave the house that day?"

"Well, it's always better if you leave everything to us, so if you don't mind I will schedule it for 2.00 until 4.00 in the afternoon. I will work on the advertising straightaway. Have a good day. Bye." She abruptly answered in a business like fashion.

That day had been a whirlwind of a day for me. I had been subject to the highs and lows of situations, the spectrum of which had left me drained. I had been living in two worlds, which were poles apart. I had been subjected to a social culture that was alien to my neighbors. In fact, I don't think any of them would frequent Lower Bridgewater for any reason. I decided to have an early night.

Lying in my comfy king-size bed in our master suite, I looked around asking myself if I would miss this house, and the comfortable life style we had nurtured there. However, before I slept I remember thinking to myself – it was the people in a home that mattered, and not the material goods they had around them, but I also acknowledged that Florence would not agree.

# Chapter 27
# Decisions

George and I spent a long weekend together. We talked a lot about the changes we would be making, however, in George's inevitable way; it was his contentions, which I was expected to accept.

I didn't know anything about Miami, I had never been there. I had seen the television show "Miami Vice", which illustrated the tall skyscrapers and proximity to the coast, which was idyllic; therefore, I had to recognize that George's plans for our future were better left in his hands.

In order to compromise the situation, he suggested I fly down to Miami with him, to see the prospective neighborhoods he had sieved out.

"We can stay in the apartment I have rented there, so you can take your time getting familiar with the place, and choosing a house. I have a driver who knows his way around; also I have assigned us to a company that knows my requirements and price bracket." Then without taking a breath, he announced, "I will let our realtor here have the keys to show people around, and June can keep the place tidy and clean."

The whole process seemed to be signed, sealed and delivered, so I was left me with just one question.

"When do you plan on leaving, George? I will have to sort out my summer clothes to pack."

"Oh, don't bother with packing too much, there are very good stores there, with the appropriate clothes for that climate. We will leave next Saturday and then I can get into work on Monday, you have nothing here to keep you from travelling, have you?"

I sat facing him, trying to assimilate all that he had said. I was put off guard by the imminence of the move; I could only shake my head as an answer.

The next day I decided to call Barbara to get an update. She had called the Social Services' Child Welfare Department, and asked for a personal interview at the school. They sent a supervisor to discuss the matter, no doubt because of her personal and professional standing in the community, and the delicate matter she had to talk about.

"The meeting went very well, and the lady understood clearly, Florence's situation. However, she did indicate that the children needed to be out of the Mother's hands as soon as possible. I really don't think we can do much more for Florence, and her family, these people have the expertise to handle this affair, and the resources needed, don't you agree?"

"Of course, that's the only thing we could do, even though Florence won't thank us for the intervention." I answered honestly.

I then went on to tell Barbara about my visit to Miami, and the reason for it, adding that I would miss her and the school profusely. She laughed at my admission, telling me I should be happy I would not have to contend with St John's woes, and instead enjoy the wonderful paradise that George was offering.

Before ending our conversation I told her I would keep in touch with her, to find out the final outcome of the pupils, and staff I had been involved with. I placed the receiver down with a heavy heart.

The next morning I discussed with June, the various chores that needed to be done while I was away. She was quick to say in an amusing way that George had instructed her already, and offered her a generous bonus as well.

"You deserve it, June," I said. "You have been more than an employee all these years, you have been my confidant, my support and best friend. I will miss you," I added, with tears in my eyes.

I was getting homesick before I had even left. I was nervous about the move into the unknown, but I had no option - I had to accept it. I busied myself packing, choosing the clothes I had worn when we went on holiday to the Bahamas. Hoping they would be appropriate, even though I realized, they were not suitable for the social occasions George had spoken about.

Saturday arrived, and in military style our movements had been affably programmed to get us to the airport, on time, and with all the necessary documentations and processes taken care of. It reeked of Glenda Morris's preparations.

The limousine arrived promptly, the driver taking care of the luggage, and politely asking if there was anything more he should put in the trunk. At the airport we were dealt with in the same courteous behavior by the Curbside Check-in people. I stood bewildered clasping my carry-on bag.

When we arrived in Miami the same polite procedures took place, there was even a well-dressed gentleman there displaying our name. He quickly diverted us to the baggage claim area to retrieve our bags, which he then collected, and escorted us to a very large limousine.

George seemed to recognize the gentleman and thanked him profusely for his punctuality, which I thought was rather overdone, but the effect was probably for my benefit, to show he was in complete control of the situation.

I looked through the window as we drove towards the city, and saw very few people walking on the street. The ones I did see were curiously holding umbrellas, although it clearly was not raining. I asked George about this oddity, and with a small snigger he told me they were protecting themselves from the heat of the sun.

I had at that point not been out of air conditioning so could not imagine how hot it was. When we got to the apartment building I got out of the car and headed for the entrance, witnessing my first experience of Miami's climate.

Once inside the grand foyer I had to shiver, the contrast was so great.
"Are you alright?" George concernedly asked.

"Yes, it's just that it is really cold in this area."

"You'll soon get use to the fact of high central air conditioning in public places, especially where the occupants have to wear formal clothes for appearance sake. Follow the man to the elevator; I want to see if I have any messages, I won't be long." George loudly instructed.

I did as I was told and meekly followed our driver. He didn't speak until we reached a large double door, on the other side of the elevator. Then to my amazement he slid a card along the lock, before escorting me into a kind of small reception area, where he put down the bags.

I fumbled for my purse to find some money for a tip, but I was unsure of the amount I should give him. I offered a twenty-dollar bill to him, but he shook his head, and with a strange foreign accent said,

"No, No Mr. Daniels has taken care of everything; I hope to see you very soon."
He went through the door into the elevator, and left me standing uncertain as to the direction I should go. I looked bewilderingly at my surroundings. The private elevator had left so I closed the large door. This area had a marble floor with expensive scatter rugs to add to the luxurious look. I was still standing there wondering which of the numerous doors I should open when the

elevator came back and George emerged through the door.

"Have you not looked around yet? Come on Mrs. Daniels let me show you our spacious apartment, and then you can tell me if it is to your liking. Just leave the bags there."

He took my hand and pulled me through one of the doors into a huge sitting room that had large picture windows on two sides. They reached from floor to ceiling, but George slid one open with one hand and told me to feast out on the magnificent ocean view.

I went through the door to a very large wrap-around patio that was complete with lavish outdoor furniture. I gazed at the spectacular sight. On one side was the ocean with boats bobbing up and down on the sparkling water; on the other side were the large skyscrapers, which were signatures of downtown Miami.

I sat breathlessly admiring the scene, taking in the cool fresh air, which I preferred to the cold air conditioning, oblivious of my husband leaving, and then returning with two glasses filled with cool orange juice.

"This is the place to get fresh squeezed orange juice, Mary, straight from the trees which grow abundantly here," he said sitting down beside me. "This is how we were meant to live, my dear, don't you agree?"

I was lost for words, so I nodded, smiled, and drank the delicious juice feeling a world away from Lower Bridgewater.

# Chapter 28
# Fresh Faces

I took advantage of my new surroundings for the next few days. Resting, reading and accepting the place I was in. The circumstances should have given me pleasure, but in fact I was not comfortable there. When I spoke to George about this, he told me it was probably due to the fact it was a rented apartment and not ours.

"Maybe it is time we bought our own place, dear. I am sure that is the answer. I have a few areas in mind, so tomorrow we will go together and explore. I have the office fully manned now, and I can leave Glenda to manage while I am away."

I had learned to accept my husband's control, and although I was not at ease with the way things were going, I had no alternative to offer.

"Should we not wait until our house sells before we purchase here?" I asked, but he quickly responded,

"Mary, please don't worry your little head about financial matters, I have everything under control. All I want from you is to choose a location, a house that you like and fill it with the appropriate furniture." Then he added as an afterthought, "I think we should leave at 10 a.m.. Is that O.K. with you?" I nodded my approval with a weak smile.

Prompt and punctual our driver arrived, dressed a little less formally than the day we arrived, but still immaculately groomed and overly courteous. George inquired if he had the list of houses Glenda had prepared for us, which he confidently answered with a heavy accent.

"Everything has been taken care of, Sir. The Realtors will greet us at each house, and Ms. Morris has spoken with them individually as regards to price. Are you ready to leave straightaway?"

Of course I was standing by ready for the task in hand, so I followed them both into the elevator, and towards yet more unexpected surprises.

We went to an area called Coral Gables, another called Pinecrest and finally towards Miami Beach's Fisher Island, a place which was reached by a ferry. Then finally we went to Star Island. All the houses we saw were mega mansions, with large cathedral ceilings, outdoor swimming pools and even maid's quarters. They were, in my opinion too large for two people and too ostentatious for my liking. Caroline and James Turner would have loved the houses, but to me they were not 'homey', and were too pretentious.

Of course, George did not agree with my judgments. He told me I had to change my outlook, and accept the fact we were in a different social standing here in Miami.

"I will be judged by my clients on my propriety, where I live, and my persona is very important for my business. For goodness sake, Mary, make up your mind, you have seen some very good potential houses, pick one."

We were back in the apartment having this conversation, so his loud antagonizing behavior towards me was not witnessed. I was tired after a day of house searching, and feeling out of my depth with the choices. I fought back the tears to answer.

"I think maybe the one on Star Island is my choice. The views from the house were similar to the ones here, which I find very calming."

"Good choice, Mary." He abruptly answered, "Star Island it will be. Also it is to be sold fully furnished, which will make our move easier and quicker. That's how we should sell our house. I will get Glenda to telephone our Realtor and arrange that."

I realized there was a lack of consideration for my 'things'. We had chosen the furniture and pictures together in our last home. We had added ornaments, throw cushions, as well as all the bits and pieces, over time. Curtains, rugs and changes to wall colors were jointly agreed. Now, suddenly, none of it mattered to George; it could be disregarded in one quick phone call by his trusting side-kick. I knew, yet again, that my opinions meant nothing in my husband's grand scale of things to come. Arguing the matter was futile.

The following day George went to work, and left me alone in the apartment. I made myself something to eat and poured myself a refreshing glass of orange juice. I took it outside to soak in the fresh sea breeze, and tried to assimilate the things that were changing for me. I needed to talk to someone whose opinion mattered to me, so I called Barbara.

I tried to sound upbeat, and first joked with her about missing the trials and tribulations of St. John's. She answered jovially,

"Oh, yes, I am sure you would swap your life in Miami for Lower Bridgewater."

The real truth was that at that moment in time I really did miss them all. My life now lacked purpose and meaning, materialistic things could not replace that feeling. Barbara wanted me to tell her all about Miami, and what I had been doing since I got there. Her curiosity for people and places she had never experienced was the sounding block I needed. I told her, in detail, about the apartment, the house hunt and even the women carrying umbrellas when it was not raining. We laughed together, and I promised to keep her up to date with the intended move.

As I ended the call I felt a knot in my stomach tighten. I gulped for air in between sipping my orange juice, and looked out at the ocean trying to find some positive thoughts, but they were eluding me. I was indifferent to the splendor around me, although I did appreciate the natural beauty of the scenery, I felt undeserving of the position I was seeing it from.

Just then I had a call from my pretentious husband, bringing me back to the realities of the situation.

"What a beautiful day to be in Paradise" was his opening remark. "I hope you are taking full advantage of the apartment, and its spectacular visage. Soak it in, Mary, forget the past, I am taking you to new horizons. I am truly breathless at the speed my business is growing here. Tonight we will be meeting the movers and shakers of Miami at a fundraiser for the potential political candidate. Go to the beauty parlor, buy yourself a pretty dress and be ready by 5p.m. Must go, enjoy the rest of your day."

The whole of this one sided conversation was said without pausing for a reaction. He spoke without taking a breath between his various statements. My facial reactions were luckily not seen, or detected, or he would have known I was not on the same page as he was. I was taken aback by this sudden jump up in our economic standing and unsure if I could, or would, find my comfort zone.

I was not enamored with the thought of shopping for a new dress, and I definitely did not want to visit any beauty parlor. The latter I could get around, however I did know that I needed to shop for a more flimsy, light fabric dress. The clothes I had brought were not suitable for Miami, so I reluctantly went out to purchase something more appropriate.

The task was not as difficult as I had imagined. Our apartment was centrally located and in walking distance to many department stores. It didn't take me long to find a suitable garment and colorful shoes to match at a bargain price.

I took a leisurely bath in the afternoon, and then spent time fixing my hair up, while leaving strands to curl naturally down. It was a style I had learned to do easily, and knew it always worked to create the look I was comfortable with. I always used a lot of moisturizer, and my complexion didn't need foundation, so a little lipstick and mascara was all I needed to finish my intended 'look'.

My outward demeanor hid my inward anxiety of the social occasion. I had no idea what 'the movers and shakers of Miami' looked like, or in fact, what in essence, the phrase meant, but I was about to find out.

# Chapter 29
# Alien Situations

The event took place on the rooftop of a distinguished Miami Beach hotel. Our trusted driver had arrived to whisk us away to the destination, where he duly dropped us off at the entrance.

I followed George, like a lap dog sticking close to its master, but all the time looking around at the gathering crowd heading for the elevators. Fortunately, my dress choice fitted in easily with the eclectic people heading towards the same function. However, I was glad I had chosen to bring my trusted silk shawl as we merged onto the garden rooftop that overlooked the ocean. The sun was setting fast making way for the spectacular moon, which lit up the sky over Miami. My thoughts were in the clouds as my husband thrust a glass of white wine into my hands, and gently whispered into my ear.

"You look amazing, dear, now just stay by my side as I mingle with these people," and then he added in a hopeful voice. "They all could be potential clients."

I was surprised how ethnically diverse the people were. Europeans, South Americans, Canadians, Chinese and even Russians mixed easily together, using the universal English language. When they spoke to each other everyone seemed at ease talking about their homeland and why they had come to Miami, and how elated they were to become citizens of America. I was fascinated with their stories, and wished, for a split second, that my good friend, Barbara, could have been there with us. This was the sort of social gathering she would have enjoyed.

My short-lived pleasure was interrupted by a voice on a microphone asking us all to look towards the raised platform set up at one end. The person on the microphone introduced a well-dressed gentleman as the prospective candidate for the upcoming political governor's race.

He spoke at length about himself, his views and his ideas for change. I blanked out his droning voice, and found myself a seat at a vacant garden table, behind the standing guests. The crowd seemed to be appreciative to his views, applauding and gesturing their support for his standpoint.

Then, to my dismay, my husband, George, joined them on the podium, and took the microphone from the announcer. He introduced himself,

"Ladies and Gentlemen, friends and colleagues, it is with great pleasure I start this fundraiser. As some of you know my company is based here in Miami, and are at you service 24/7. I am honored to start the ball rolling with $100,000. Who will join me with their donations? Please come to the ladies here who are ready and waiting to receive your commitments. Thank you."

I was horrified, stunned. George had just donated $100.000. I was speechless, bewildered and wished the ground would just swallow me up. The audience were applauding, and turning towards me as George walked stately by them to sit down next to me. I quickly excused myself to find a restroom to escape.

As I was returning to the table I noticed a large crowd had gathered around George, who was distributing his business cards and chatting animatedly with them. I stood back to watch this unusual incident, and couldn't help noticing that the people around him were vying with each other to reach a card. I waited until most of them had left the table before I joined my husband. He was in euphoria, and in an exhilarating voice said,

"I really should have brought more cards, but I suppose they now know who I am, and will get in touch with the office."

I nodded my head in platitude to his remark and asked if we could return home as I had a very bad headache and felt sickly.

"That's because you haven't eaten dear, shall we go down to the restaurant here in the hotel, I'm sure they will be accommodating?"

I didn't really want to drag the evening out, but I knew George was in his element, and wanted to continue to be the focus of attention, so I consented.

After a large tip was presented by George to the Maître d' we were led to a table for two near the window overlooking the ocean. It wasn't long before other guests from the fundraiser entered the restaurant, and quite obviously made their way past our table to make polite conversation with George.

He was totally enamored by all this attention, and continually repeated that he would be in touch with them tomorrow. One gentleman put his finger at the side of his nose and winked, which was a gesture I didn't understand, but I saw George wink back.

I didn't bring up the subject of the donation, even though I was curious about the size of it. Nevertheless, George eagerly told me later, on the way home in the car, that it was money well spent. I did not have the courage to pry further, although in retrospect I wish I had.

The next few weeks went by in a whirlwind of changes. Our home was sold furnished, and a few personal items miraculously appeared in boxes at the apartment in Miami. George informed me that Glenda had flown back and, with the help of June, they had emptied my closet and drawers. I was at least happy about the fact that June had participated.

The buyer had purchased everything including the pots, pans, silverware and china, together with the crystal glasses, pictures and all the furnishings. They had apparently been overseas, and had returned to the States with just their clothes.

"I think it has all turned out for the best, Mary. I wanted to buy more unique things for our new home. You will enjoy shopping for exceptional effects to enhance the place."

He saw the dismay in my face so quickly added, "if you are not comfortable doing that, I can always bring in an interior designer, there are plenty good ones here in Miami."

"Yes," I answered meekly, "maybe that would be a better option."

# Chapter 30
# Finding Solitude

The move to Star Island was done very perfunctorily; the whole process was taken out of my hands by people my husband called 'professionals'. This house did not feel like a home to me, but more like a stage set waiting for the actors to perform.

It was a mausoleum mansion far too big for two people. Over the following weeks I made myself a small retreat at the back of the house overlooking the water. I called it my study, which George found an apt title for the smallest room in the house. I bought accessories that made me feel comfortable, and relaxed. A place I could withdraw to, and forget the opulence and kitsch that surrounded it.

George led a very busy life style, continually working his business both in his professional and social life. I felt more and more like a garnish he could use when needed, far away from the closeness and companionship we once had. His clients and associates were of one kind, pompous, brash and materialistic men and women, who I had no empathy with. Their hollow misconception of me, did not adhere to my ego, but it did concern George.

"What's wrong with you, Mary?" He angrily asked, "Could you try to be more accommodating with 'my people'. It is important you play your part, and give me the support, and backing I need to be successful. It is essential they perceive a happy devoted couple whom they want to emulate. Can you at least join me a little more on these social occasions?"

I listened intently to his demands, but answered him with the opposite to my true feelings.

"I'm sorry I am not coming up to your expectations, (living up to your façade). I will make a conscious effort (I will create the pretense) to join you more and sustain your standing in this society."

He brushed his cheek against mine, but tightly held my shoulders so as not to surrender his composure to my yearning for affection.

So it was that I give in to his demanding requests, and joined him on a few of his social events. Fortunately for me, his new in-house lawyer was a like minded young recruit, who loved sport, and also had family contacts in the political world. Two areas where George loved to spread his benevolent funds, and advertise his business with free marketing from the press. His face was becoming more and more familiar on the television news, and in the newspaper. I was relieved I didn't need, nor care, for the notoriety that accompanied those press releases. I was too bashful to open myself up to scrutiny by the media, and thankful that his newfound friend and side-kick reveled in it as much as George did. This young man had replaced me, consequently I was off the hook, and able to pursue my own areas of interest.

I decided to offer my services as a volunteer at "The Deering Estate". This is a beautiful mansion house and museum full of precious antiquities that bring people from around the world to see. The 444 acres on Biscayne Bay has been preserved very tastefully, and its position overlooking the water is an ideal spot for tourists.

After a brief induction period, I was placed alongside a very knowledgeable volunteer, who gave me a lot of encouragement and insight to overcome my primary fear of not being conversant with the many questions people asked. He had a simple answer to that dilemma –

"Just say you will find out the answer at the end of the tour, as it was something you would not like to guess at, and then continue the tour giving the group details that you are sure about."

Before long I regained my positive self-confidence. My voice projection was a skill I had learned back in the Drama Club in my University days, and my ability to research had been tested at St John's, therefore, the task was a pleasurable one, which gave me my self-esteem back. After a few weeks I was a fully-fledged tour guide who loved her newfound occupation.

I had found a project that filled my time, and gave me satisfaction. I enjoyed the research into Charles Deering and his climb to wealth. He was a philanthropist who appreciated the arts, and saved many antiques from being destroyed from war zones around the world. He was my kind of person, someone who wanted to share his good fortune with others. His possessions were valuable not in a monetary way, but in preserving them from being lost or damaged.

George seemed to be happy I had found my niche in Miami society. I think it fitted his agenda when he was discussing me with his clients. The importance of the Estate that belongs now to

Miami-Dade County was not lost to George's party line.

"My wife is a very intelligent person, especially in antiquities and historical events here in Miami," was a frequent line of his. Personally I believe my husband had no idea who Charles Deering was, or what his legacy entailed. However, as long as it made him happy, as well as me, then I was content with the state of affairs.

Nonetheless, I was concerned about his appearance. He looked terribly drawn and tired. He was drinking more and eating less.

I was troubled about the amount of time he was spending on the telephone, even when he had come home from work, or from an event. One night, after he had made a rather long conversation on the phone, I tentatively approached him with my concerns.

He rested back on the sofa, and shared his present situation with me. Apparently, Brad Portman, his partner in New York, had collapsed, and had been taken to hospital with a very bad heart attack. Vicky, his wife was reporting to George each day, but the doctors were not very hopeful he would fully recover.

"I am really worried, Mary. Not only is he the mainstay of our office in New York, but he is the only person there who personally connects to our clients, they are his customers. The rich investors of New York are nothing like the ones down here. I think I need to go there and find out for myself what is going on at our office. If possible, I need to speak to Brad; that is, if he is well enough, and also see if I can persuade the clients to stay with our company."

He rested back and sipped his drink. I rose from my chair and joined him on the sofa placing my hands on his.

"Of course you must go. He is our friend as well as a business partner." I waited for a minute before continuing, "Would you like me to come with you? Perhaps I could console Vicky, and help her somehow."

He turned to me and with a weak smile he told me that Vicky's sister was there with her, and she seemed to have taken over the domestic affairs. After a few minutes of silence he thanked me for the offer, and then assured me that I was to contact Glenda if I had any problems, and couldn't get in touch with him in New York. I maintained the silence.

Two days later George left for New York together with his young lawyer, who was eager to spread his wings in the 'Big Apple'. George was equally enthusiastic to test his ability in a different environment, hoping he would come up to his high expectations. I was relieved that once more this young man had stepped into my shoes, so enabling me to continue in my newly found occupation. Actually, I was content to be left to my own devices, away from the justifications and restrictions my husband required. I could be, for a short time at least, plain Mary Daniels, instead of the wife of George Daniels, the well-known entrepreneur.

I loved my job. Every day was different. The tourists, who joined my groups, were always very diverse and widely varied. They appreciated and respected my insight into that wonderful place, and their enthusiasm bounced off me. Even the groups of school children were a pleasure to guide. I wished in my heart, that some of the pupils of St John's could have joined them to experience the grandeur; unfortunately that occurrence was far from being practical.

I pushed the thought to the back of my mind, and resolved to count my blessings. I was in a beautiful location; my husband and I were both healthy, moreover we were each doing jobs that gave us satisfaction. What more was there to wish for?

# Chapter 31
# Lonely and Alone

I received frequent phone calls from George, updating me on the situation in New York, and therefore, to my relief I did not have to get in touch with the unfailing Glenda.

I was sorry to hear that Brad's health had deteriorated, and although he was back home with Vicky, he was not functioning as well as he did before. Ultimately, they both came to the conclusion that it would be advisable for Brad to retire. Vicky especially thought the job was too stressful, and he should now take things easy and enjoy a more leisurely life.

I really anticipated that this decision would frustrate my husband, and hinder the running of his business there in New York, but I was mistaken. George told me that, Alan Price, which was the name of his young attorney, had taken the challenge of contacting Brad's most important clients, and persuaded them to stay with the company.

"The young whippersnapper, had actually wined and dined the most important ones, and obviously impressed them with his candor and fortitude. I am very impressed by the young fellow, Mary," he declared. "I am thinking of letting him stay here in New York, there is a strong team to support him, and I am impressed with his new approach."

"Well, you know best, dear, I'm sure you will make the right decision." I proffered, but added, "How long will you be up there? I fully understand you must have a lot to sort out."

He seemed relieved that I was not pushing him to return, in fact, I sensed he was enjoying this young man's company, and the opportunities and openings that only New York could offer. His demeanor and attitude to work and pleasure sounded like he was back to his old self. Impulsive impetuous George.

"I'm really needed here, there is a lot of logistics that only I can set in place, and I can't just throw the young man in at the deep end, although I think his fresh new approach will pay dividends for us all." Then he added, as an afterthought, "Brad and Vicky send their regards, dear, take care." He had ended the conversation.

Truthfully, I had developed my own routine. I enjoyed a laid-back breakfast of coffee and croissants on the patio. Reading the morning newspaper without needing to comment on the articles, was a bonus. I enjoyed choosing an outfit to wear for my job, and putting a little make-up on with the attention it needed. Pleasing me in the mirror was the additional benefit.

My colleagues were mostly older people, retirees who were keenly caught up in staying active and involved. However, one man seemed oddly out of place, he looked far too young and fit to be guiding tour groups around. I had only caught a glimpse of him from time to time, as I had a set place to start and end my tours.

I was told by one of the other guides that he mostly did the outdoor events and he organized the special weekend activities, he was known as Mr. Terry, although she didn't know if that was his first or last name.

One day when I was in the coffee lounge he came in, and sat at my table. He introduced himself and asked my name. It turned out he was part of the permanent staff management, also it was his job to supervise the events planning. I was amazed to find out the number and diversity of events that did take place. I knew that weddings were held there, but not cabaret concerts, kids' camps, vintage auto shows, holiday events and even art days.

"My, you are a busy guy, but I expect it gives you a great deal of pleasure."

"It does." He said with a smile. "Tell me what do you do here? You look too young to be one of the volunteer guides."

It was my turn to smile, as I told him that I was, and thanked him for his compliment. He was very easy to talk to, and from that day on, we met at the same time each day for coffee. In fact it became the time of the day I looked forward to most.

Choosing an outfit to wear each day became more important, and I gradually began to feel young and virile inside. I felt my appearance and manner were more up beat and lighthearted. I enjoyed his attention to me as well as his interesting conversation.

I hadn't mentioned I was married, in fact I had told him very little about myself. Our conversations were mainly about the upcoming events. He asked my view about tasks he was undertaking, and seemed to value my observations. It was great to have someone respect my opinions; it was a part of me that had recently been surrendered.

Then one day, he asked me if I would like to have dinner with him. I was speechless, and regretful that I had maybe led him on to believe I was available. However, a part of me was longing for affection, and intimacy, and I wondered if a simple dinner date could fill the void. I was enjoying my daytime liaisons, but they were in the midst of contemporaries, not in a clandestine location. I simply said,

"I'm sorry Terry, but I have to decline. It's not possible."

"Oh, I'm sorry I didn't mean to put you in a difficult position. I just thought we could have more time together, I enjoy your company so much."

"I enjoy your company too. I hope we can continue our lunchtime conversations, I do get a real lot of pleasure from them."

There was a pregnant pause in our conversation, as we both sipped our coffee, alerting our joint gaze to the coffee cups. Finally, Terry rose from the table, telling me he must get back to work as he had a lot to do. I smiled and nodded my head; this gesture was a substitute for the words I couldn't convey.

That evening I deliberately decided to make a phone call to George, I was missing him, plus I felt guilty for enjoying another man's company. I used my cell and called his hotel room. It rang for some considerable time, then, to my astonishment a women's voice came on.

"Do you realize how long we have been waiting for room service?" she shouted down the phone.

I threw my phone across the room.

# Chapter 32
# Pulling at my Heartstrings

George returned home the following week, after spending six long weeks away. I wanted to approach the subject of the woman in his room, but I had consoled myself that it was maybe a secretary or a co-worker from the office working late. Whatever the reason was, I knew George would have a plausible excuse, and my reasonable question would be turned around to being a question of inquisitive meddling into his corporate life. I was feeling a real disconnect between my life at Deering and my home life. I should have felt happy my husband was home, but instead I was intimidated by his raucous manner, as well as his constant boasting.

That night at dinner I was bombarded by tales of political fundraising events, and hunting and fishing trips with the wealthy New Yorkers. He said things of people who he had wined and dined with who were 'famous', but their names were unfamiliar to me, so I failed to be impressed.

George sensed I was not responding to his accomplishments, and once more he admonished me.

"You know Mary, you need to support me more, or at least be pleased I am achieving 'our' wealth and fortune through 'my' hard work." He thumbed the table with his fist as he shouted the two words.

I flinched at his action, and with tears in my eyes I submissively answered. "But I am grateful, George that you work so hard, you deserves to be rewarded in a way that satisfies you, it's just that I am not comfortable with worshiping wealth. The world seems too disjointed. I am not wholly converted to the shallow values the rich seem to reflect."

I knew as soon as I had finished my sentence that I had started an argument which I was not going to win. His tirade of justifications ranged from the rich being the ones who enter the halls of justice, finance, education, health and politics with the advantage of security. On the other hand he thought the poor were idle hangers on, who contributed nothing to enhance our society.

Finally I left the table with a feeble excuse,

"I'm sorry George, but I'm tired and I am sorry we…er I, don't enjoy the same things anymore, but I respect your hard work and resilience. I could never have the same stamina and determination that you have." I went around the table to kiss his forehead then I told him I loved him.

He held my hand and apologized for being so abrupt, "I'll stay here a little longer and sip my bourbon, I need to fathom a few things out before I go to bed."

I went upstairs alone once more.

The next morning I was surprised to see George sitting at the kitchen table sipping coffee, and reading the newspaper. He didn't seem to be in a hurry, so I wondered if he was staying home.

"No, dear, but remember I am the boss, and I don't need to be accountable to anyone. I have a very good staff, which is well trained. As long as I keep bringing the clients in, they can deal with the paperwork." He said not looking up from his newspaper.

I looked at the clock, and realized I had to rush to get to my job in time for my first guided tour. I asked if he needed me for anything, but just as I was walking out, he called me back.

"I want you to be back in time to get ready for the reception we are going to this evening."

I was confused so I asked where we were going, because he hadn't told me about any function. To my dismay he told me we would be returning to my workplace, but in a 'patron's' capacity.

"We are going to the Deering Estate for a fundraiser for our future Governor, I am sure I mentioned this to you last night. It will be a very positive move for me, as I have been out of the social circuit for quite a time. However, I do have a lot to say about the people I was with in New York, and that should impress a lot of them." Then he added without any real expectation of my response. "Keep up the good work, dear, and don't be late, I will see you later."

As I drove to work I found my hands were gripping the wheel tightly. I was breathing heavily, and becoming impatient with other drivers. I was inwardly furious, incensed at the uncaring attitude of my husband. He had only been back one day, and already he was preaching at me, authorizing my time, also expecting me to have no response to his requirements.

I couldn't see a way out of my situation. Thankfully I was able to be myself, and enjoy my day with people who were responsive to my words and knowledge. I truly felt valued and respected doing my job; it was a worthwhile profession, moreover the appreciation I received from the tourists made me feel good.

My ego during the day was quickly deflated when I returned home, and saw my husband dressed immaculately, in a grey suit and tie.

"You have cut it fine, dear. You have very little time to get ready. I don't want to be the first to arrive, but I seriously don't want to be the last. Can you spruce yourself up in under an hour?" He asked while having a conversation on his cell.

Of course I was able to change from Mary Daniels to submissive Mrs. Daniels in under an hour, and made the journey in our company driven car in silence. I hoped and prayed that none of my colleagues would be around in the evening; in some way I wished my two lives could remain separate.

My wish was not granted. Standing at the entrance greeting and directing the guests was Terry. I wanted the ground to swallow me up, thank goodness George was holding my arm tightly, which supported my weak knees. At first I thought maybe Terry had not recognized me as he pleasantly smiled and made no comment. He directed us, along with two other couples who were behind us, to go through the first double doors.

The room we entered was full of round tables, however very few people were seated; they were walking around from group to group. Waiters mingled between them with trays full of drinks. I was unsure if I sat down it would be the wrong thing to do, so I followed George from group to group, smiling politely, and nodding in support of his egotistical remarks. I perfunctorily moved at his side, shaking hands courteously after every introduction. I was relieved when the announcement was made for us to be seated.

A light meal was served along with wine for which I was glad, as I didn't have to join in the conversations. However, it didn't stop George. He had no problem doing both; I think he had had plenty of practice. The evening dragged on with speeches of support, but I found a break, and excused myself to go to the ladies' restroom.

I went through the doors, and was looking around for a sign, when a familiar voice called my name. I turned and saw Terry walking towards me.

"I thought it was you when you came in. Is that your husband you're with, or a friend?" He said as he stopped in front of me.

I gulped, and then replied, "Yes it is my husband, Terry, He has just returned from New York, where he has been working,"

Behind us was a bench, so I was glad to sit down to gain my composure, to calm the churning in my stomach. Terry joined me, thankfully at a safe distance. We were both staring at the floor, and not at each other.

"Pardon me saying, Mary, but you don't look happy he is back. In fact I have never seen you with such a morbid expression. The Mary I know is full of delight, and amusing to be with. I loved to hear your positive suggestions about some of the problems I had with my events." He hesitated for a moment before saying; "I suppose I blew it when I asked you out to dinner. I'm sorry about that, but I hope we can still be friends."

My impulse was to say 'of course' and tell him I also enjoyed his company a lot. Fortunately, the door from the reception opened, and two women came out, they asked if I knew where the restroom was. Terry stood up, and indicated the direction they should go. When they had gone out of sight I stood up, and simply said, "Maybe I will see you in the café? I am not sure of my schedule, but my break will probably be the same time of the day. I can't stay to talk now, Terry, my husband will be wondering where I am."

"Of course, enjoy the rest of your evening. By the way was everything O.K. with the set up in there, and the service? I'm always a bit nervous when the 'big wigs' book the room."

"Everything is splendid, you did a good job. Bye Terry." I walked away without looking back. I could sense his disappointment, as I left him awkwardly watching me go back to join my husband. I had to pull myself together, forcing myself back to reality. The man on the bench was utopia for me; he had to remain just a colleague, I was, after all, a married woman.

# Chapter 33
# Getting it Straight

I returned to the function, and back to my seat. The speeches had finished, so many of the audience were up on their feet and moving from table to table. I looked around for George, and spotted him talking and laughing with a large group of listeners on the other side of the room.

I sat at the empty table and sipped the rest of my wine, hoping my husband would sense I was ready to leave. Regrettably, he was in no hurry, in fact I think he had forgotten I was even with him. He moved on to another group of people who were nearer to our table, and began again to engage them into his enticing discourse. I watched him pass round his business cards, but I noticed he was indicating to them that he had no more left, so I stood up and turned towards him. Thankfully, he joined me.

"I suppose you are ready to go, dear, and I think it is a good time for us to leave. Better to keep the punters hungry for more information, their expectations for a potential big deal grows in their minds. My telephone will be ringing off the hook tomorrow. I know that for sure."

On the way back home his vain conversation begged for no comment, so mercifully he was satisfied with a smile, and a nod from me. Our recent habit of me going to bed straightaway and George pouring himself a nightcap was the routine that night. It suited us both.

I lay awake tossing and turning trying hard to get my racing mind to stop. The vision of kind, caring Terry, was in sharp contrast to inconsiderate George. One was unobtainable, and the other unchangeable. Eventually, I drifted off to sleep.

As expected, George was very busy. Even when he was home, he was constantly on the telephone, our conversations were short, and matter of fact, mainly on the subject of whether he would be eating dinner at home, and if so at what time.

I was thankful I had the job at Deering; the company was good and the situation stimulating. I made a determined effort to go to the café each lunch time, but for days there was no sign of Terry. I asked the cashier, casually if she had seen him; however she told me that he hadn't been in the café for over a week, which was extraordinary.

I tried to push the disappointment out of my head; after all I did have many other colleagues to spend time with, although my conversations with them were enjoyable, but insignificant. I tried to put this strange feeling of emptiness out of my churning, unsettled stomach. It was a feeling of rejection, of loss, yet I knew I had never had the ownership in the first place. Terry was, and always had been just a friend, with whom I got pleasure from having conversations. I told myself I needed to stop acting like a pining schoolgirl, and face reality. Mrs. Mary Daniels was a disillusioned woman having a mid-life crisis.

I returned from the restroom ready for the afternoon groups that were always large, noisy and gratifying. They would distract my thoughts from straying into restricted beliefs.

Weeks went by in a monotonous way. Although I did like working in the day, my evenings were tedious. Much of this was my own fault as I had opted out of going with George to many of his social events. Then one night he asked me a question.

"Perhaps you should think of cutting down on your volunteering work, then you wouldn't be so tired. You need to do something different. How about you come with me to New York for a few days? I have to make a visit there next week, and I know you like the art galleries and theater there.

You could also do a little shopping to keep occupied. Then in the evenings we could have an intimate dinner together. How does that sound?"

I smiled and went towards him, and for a long time in coming we caressed. I told him it was just what I needed. I meant every word.

We left for New York the following week. In fact, I was ready to have a change of scene; furthermore there are no two more contrasting cities than Miami and New York. Getting out of the heat and humidity to the cool fall days of New York would be a relief; also the change of pace from laid back to bustling was something I felt ready for.

"Will you be alright occupying yourself during the day, Mary?" George asked over breakfast.

"Of course I will." Was my reply, "I will get a taxi to where-ever I decide to go. There are plenty available outside the hotel."

We were going to be in New York for a week, so I was eager to plan my days to get the best possible experience from the little time I had. The hotel concierge was very obliging, and with his help my days were filled with uplifting venues.

Just as George had promised, our evenings were spent quietly together, enjoying the different cuisines offered in this diverse city.

Consequently, when the week came to a close I was over and done with my infatuation with Terry. I was appreciative of my husband, and the possibilities he showered on me. The opportunity to be in such a vibrant place, with a caring husband, was not lost on me.

As we flew back to our home in Miami, I hugged my husband's arm, as we sipped our champagne in the luxury of the aircraft's first class seats. At that time I was happy to be in the secure, reassuring company of my partner, my husband. That is something every woman searches for, and if it is there, then it should be cosseted. I vowed on that day I would be more responsive to George's requests, along with being grateful for his work ethic that allowed us to live life to the fullest.

I also wondered why I was pushing myself to acknowledge this state of affairs. He had chosen to be the sole provider, and kept me at arm's length away from his business dealings. I had tried on many occasions to ask about his work; however I got only careful, decisive answers.

"You sit back and enjoy the fruits of my labor, dear. I need you to be my social butterfly; that is all I ask."

The ache in my stomach responded in my head that I was never a socialite, and certainly was not a butterfly, however, I was trapped.

# Chapter 34
# Surprise Toys

In the months that followed our New York visit, George started to acquire many expensive 'toys' that really were too pretentious for my liking. The first was a Lamborghini, which quite frankly was too sleek and tight to fit George's expanding large frame. He showed it off at every opportunity.

"This autobile, my friends, is a Lamborghini Veneno, a very limited edition that can reach speeds of 220 miles per hour. What do you think?"

Most of the people he showed it off to, were very impressed; however, I could not imagine any place he could test this claim out, except on a race track. I couldn't imagine myself, or George, squeezing ourselves into it, and in any case, he always liked to be driven everywhere. It was yet another collection piece.

After that car, came another one. Perhaps a more suitable one for George's stature, it was a Rolls-Royce Ghost, so I was told. He would go to work in that, enjoying the luxury of sitting in the back seat as his driver played chauffeur, to enhance his self-esteem.

The toys grew in the next year; so much so, we had to have another large garage built. I say garage, but it was more like a warehouse. A Harley-Davison Dodge motor bike, stood next to a 1910 Vintage Winchester bike, and they were surrounded by even more vintage cars as time went by.

I could not see the rationale in this vehicle collection, but I was informed by my husband that they were a very good insurance policy if we had an economic downturn. Furthermore, he got a great deal of pleasure from showing them to his ever increasing clients and acquaintances.

I continued to get my happiness and satisfaction from my volunteering work at Deering so; once more I could feel us growing apart. Then one morning, to my delight, I received a call from Barbara. She told me she was leaving St John's, to take a position in Japan.

"You know I have always liked to travel and see new cultures, so now is my opportunity. I am so excited, Mary." Then before I could congratulate her she went on to say that she was going to take a short holiday before going to Japan, and would love to come to see me in Miami.

I should have been so happy to receive my good friend in my home, but truthfully, I was embarrassed and uncomfortable welcoming her to this pseudo house where I now lived. I had to think fast in order to give a plausible excuse.

"I am so glad for you, Barbara. They will truly miss you at St John's, but you deserve the chance to spread your wings and enjoy a new life. You know I would love to invite you down here, but we are having some major renovations done that the builder says is going well, but I am sure will take another 6 weeks. Is it possible for us to meet somewhere, maybe New York, if you can manage it? My husband goes there a lot so his company could accommodate us, so you would only have to pay for your fare."

I waited anxiously for her response, hoping it would be positive. However, I knew Barbara did nothing spontaneously. Finally, I heard her chuckle, before she answered,

"You know, Mary, I have always wanted to visit New York, moreover, this year is going to be my time for taking chances, for experiencing all the things I have procrastinated about for too long.

Could we meet at the end of the month for a long weekend, does that fit into your schedule?"

I told her about my volunteering job, and how I could manage to take time off. I also added that I would take care of all the planning, and then let her know the logistics for her to approve of.

"That's my Mary, the organization queen. It will be great whatever you decide; I have utter faith in your decisions," she said with a giggle. "Just let me know the dates, and place where we will meet, then we can go from there. I am so excited; I can't wait to see you. Bye for now, take care."

Her abrupt end to the call dismayed me, but on the other hand I had to accept tht she was a working woman with responsibilities to take care of.

When I told George about my planned visit, he was surprisingly positive about me spending time with my good friend Barbara, whom he amazingly recalled, had been an acquaintance of mine before we came to Miami. Fearing I would loose his concentration on my affairs, I asked him if I could use the company's accommodation contacts.

"Of course, Mary, I will get Glenda to sort everything out for you."

"I would rather do the planning myself, George. I just need a list of recommended places from her."

"Aar well," he sighed. "I think you should call her for all the information you need, and then I will be happy to pick up the tab when you have decided."

I wanted this to be my farewell gift to Barbara; I had no intention for it to be George's contribution. I only needed help with hotel locations, then I would look on the internet to make sure we didn't stay where George and his company were known. His flamboyant behavior when we were last in New York was something I didn't want Barbara to be exposed to. It was better for me to be incognito, so we could enjoy ourselves in our own way.

During the days that followed I was immersed in selfishly doing the things I enjoyed most. Working at Deering during the day, and planning my trip to New York, in every other spare minute I got. My husband seemed to be so busy himself that we very rarely got together, even at mealtimes. At that time it seemed to suit us both, also I was eagerly looking forward to my time away. The moments I spent preparing and scheduling our program of events was, I know, just as exciting as the trip itself was going to be.

Barbara and I had the same tastes and expectations so it was not hard for me to anticipate if she would enjoy the places I chose. My only setback was cutting down on the choices because of the time factor. Eventually I had to talk to Barbara so we could agree together on the ones to leave out.

Over a long phone call that was full of laughter and friendly snipes, we came to a mutual agreement on the places to leave out. I was in such a happy mood as I went into the kitchen to make myself a drink that I was not aware, immediately, of George sitting at the kitchen table. He was stooped over, his face between his hands, and his body was shaking.

"Are you alright, George? Are you sick?" I asked going towards him. I put my hands on his bent shoulders trying to control his shaking.

"Do you want me to call a Doctor? George, talk to me. What do you want me to do?"

"You can't do anything." He said looking up at me. "I have had a shock, that's all. Its work related, I will sort it out."

"Would you like a hot drink or some cold water?" I offered.

He didn't answer me straight away, but went out and came back with a large whisky in his hand.

"It's just that I have been working a lot lately, I suppose I am worn out or coming down with something." Then after taking a drink from his glass he responded. "Maybe, I should go to New York with you, and take some time out."

I was dumbfounded, thunderstruck and speechless. Barbara had never met George, and I really didn't want her to either. I struggled to find the words, but eventually after making my coffee I took my mug to the table and sat down.

We sat facing each other like two strangers in a café struggling to find a polite conversation. Finally, I tried to give him a sincere answer.

"George, this is a ladies-only trip. My good friend is leaving the States to work in Japan, and this is going to be the last time I will see her face to face. You would be bored to tears with our company. Why don't you take the time off, and get out of Miami yourself for a while?"

Thankfully, my suggestion seemed to bring a sparkle to his eyes, then after taking another large gulp of his whisky, he smiled and nodded his head in agreement.

Relieved that I had found a solution to my dilemma, I excused myself, and told him I was taking my coffee upstairs to read my travel brochures in bed.

"That's fine dear, I have to make some calls myself to arrange things. I will be up shortly."

# Chapter 35
# Unforeseen Changes

The morning of my departure for New York came with the added bonus of having breakfast, sitting together at the table, with my husband. It was eerily pleasant, and somewhat unfamiliar from our usual snatch and grab kind of meal. Normally, we each went around the kitchen, individually making toast, coffee, and eating it, on the go, as we hurriedly centered on getting to work, knowing that the rush hour traffic would be horrendous.

That morning, he was very attentive and told me to enjoy the company of a good friend, and to remember not to scrimp on the finances. He would make sure Glenda would be available, if needed.

When the taxi arrived he waved me off from the door after a long embrace in the hallway. I have to admit I was ready to get out of Miami for a while, and immerse myself in the cultural delights of New York, so I hastily got into the taxi. I was so intent on making sure the driver knew my destination and terminal gate that I didn't look back.

The few days I spent with Barbara were memorable in many ways. I can recall a lot of mutual appreciation of cultural antiquities. Broadway shows that made us laugh and cry, holding back no emotion of restraint or embarrassment from each other. In the evening we recalled the events of the day over comfort food, and childish laughter.

"I have never had so much fun, Mary." Barbara said on our last evening together. "I have been able to be myself, and not 'the Principal'. This has been the ideal way to spend my final days in the U.S. You have made this possible, and I will never forget you."

I answered quickly holding her hand over the table, and fighting back the tears. "This has also been beneficial for me, Barbara. I needed the time away so I could recharge myself."

"Is everything O.K. with you and George?" she asked, squeezing my hand, and looking straight into my watering eyes.

I gulped, giving myself time to find the right answer, but I couldn't explain. It was difficult to put into plain words what the problem was, especially to a good friend who had never married.

Eventually, I told her it was just that I felt that George and I were growing apart.

"Maybe it's my fault for not being supportive of his entrepreneurial ventures. I have tried, but it is not my world." I said speaking aloud my inner thoughts. Barbara just continued to listen with no reaction, so I continued. "The people and events that he wishes me to be part of are alien to me. I don't feel comfortable in their company. I realize now I have probably been selfish, and I must try harder if I want to save our marriage."

We sat in silence appreciating the fact that we both could confide in each other, truthfully, without analysis or comment. I was glad I could get my feelings out in the open; I had suppressed them long enough.

Finally Barbara sat back and said, "Mary, we are being too miserable, this is our last night together. Tomorrow will be a new start for us both. Let's not spoil the time we have had together. I feel ready to face my new life head on, and you have always had this quality. I suggest we go back to the hotel and have a night-cap drink at the bar, furthermore I am not taking a 'no' from you," she said with a big grin.

The next day it was hard for us both to say 'Goodbye'. Barbara had no forwarding address, but would make sure to contact me when she was settled. We reluctantly separated at the airport to go to our specific gates, looking back one last time for a final wave, and a nod of the head.

The short flight back to Miami gave me the time to build up my positive mindset to renew and refresh my marriage. I looked down at the skyline of my new adoptive city; its fresh and cosmopolitan vibes seemed to welcome me as we landed.

I saw no driver awaiting my arrival, but I quickly refused to question with any negative reasons. I got into a taxi and headed home. I walked in, and left my suitcase in the hallway, I was ready for a drink of my favorite tea. I shivered as I waited for the kettle to boil, but realized that the air-conditioning was blasting too much cold air for my comfort. This had always been a controversial point between George and me. However, I went to the control to set it to a more reasonable temperature for me.

I went back into the kitchen, and glanced at the wall clock. It was early evening so I decided to pick up the phone to tell George I was back, safe and sound.

I called his cell phone, but I only got his answering machine. Grudgingly I called Glenda's extension at the office. Again, it went through to the answering machine. I busied myself for the next few hours catching up on menial tasks around the house, and emptying my suitcase. I spent some time looking at my mementoes of New York, and separating my clothes into clean and dirty piles, before deciding to shower and have an early night. I was exhausted from my visit, but it was pleasurable fatigue that enabled me to quickly sink into the pillows and sleep.

The next morning I woke up to realize that George had not been home. I thought maybe he had made up his mind to take a trip on his own, as he had suggested, so I decided to let him chill out, without being bothered by a fussing wife.

I let another day go by. Then my curiosity took advantage of me, and I again called George's cell. It rang and rang with no answering machine coming on this time; I had no alternative but to call Glenda.

She was very officious and unhelpful, stating only in that sickly condescending manner that Mr. Daniels was on business overseas. I answered back, in my snooty voice, asking her to be kind enough to furnish me with a contact number or e-mail address.

The line went silent. Then in a more nervous voice she told me she was not in a position to disclose that to me.

"What do you mean woman!" I screamed, "That is my husband I am inquiring about, tell me immediately or I will call the police that he is a missing person."

She coughed and spluttered for a little while until she finally said,

"I will get Mr. Daniels to call you today, immediately, very soon." Then she added in a whispered voice. "There is no need to go to that extreme, no need at all."

I smashed the receiver down, and took a deep breath. What was all the secrecy about, I wondered, but I had no choice but to wait for a call from my husband for an explanation.

It was an agonizing wait of four hours.. As each hour went by my emotions were taking a roller coaster ride. Had he left me? Was he hurt, and didn't want me to know, and then worry? Which hospital? Should I call the police to find out? Why did Glenda think I was over-reacting? Was I over-reacting – then the telephone rang.

It was George. I tried with all the gumption I could muster to be matter of fact.

"Hallo, dear, are you O.K.? I just wanted to tell you I was back in Miami." I said.

"That's good. Did you have a great trip with your friend?"

I stopped myself from answering his question, but instead I asked. "Did you take a trip out of Miami? I was worried when I didn't see you here."

"Well, I had some business to do out of the States, and I thought I would have finished it by now, but it's taking longer than I thought. Don't concern yourself, dear. I should be back soon. Overseas business does not go at the pace it does back home. Please bear with me, and I am sure Glenda will keep you informed. Bye for now." The line went dead.

I didn't know what to think. Where was my husband? Why was he being so secretive with me? However, he indicated that Glenda was knowledgeable about his whereabouts. I was insulted. Glenda Morris was more conversant, and up to date on my husband's situation, also the matter seemed to be quite acceptable to them both.

I made myself a cup of calming tea so I could take stock of this state of affairs. As I sipped the tea I tried to look at the matter in a reasonable and level-headed way. George was working abroad, which was a realistic thing for him to do, as he always wanted to extend his business further afield. It was usual for his secretary to take care of the logistics of his travels, so maybe I was over-responding to this situation. I decided to accept circumstances, and enjoy this added freedom it gave me.

A whole week went by without any calls from either George or his trusted secretary. My enjoyment of time to myself was turning into frustration for his lack of consideration and concern to bring me into the picture. I needed to call Glenda for an update without sounding like a wimp, after all this wasn't the first time my husband had left Miami to do business.

"Hi Glenda, Mary here," I said in a customary tone. "I wondered if you could tell me when George will be back in Miami. We have had an invite to a dinner party, and I want to know if we should accept." I lied, hoping for a positive response.

"Hallo Mary. How are you doing dear?" She answered in a caustic manner. "Have you not heard from George?"

I wanted to swear at this irritating woman – why would I call her if I had heard from George. I needed to keep my composure if I was to get any information from her.

"Well, actually I have not heard from him, I suppose he is very busy with this new project to find the time. I just need to know a date, and then I can tell our friends if the dinner is possible or not."

I waited, and waited, with no answer. "Hallo, Glenda, are you still there?' I said, unsure of her silence.

"Oh I am sorry Mary. I was consulting his calendar to see if I could answer your question. Actually, I don't have a date of his return just now; however I will keep you well-versed of his future plans as soon as I know. I'm sorry, Mary, but I have an international call on my other line, and it could be your husband. I'll call you back as soon as I have the information you need."

I was left standing, holding the receiver in disbelief. Had I been given the brush off? Was she really going to keep me in the loop? Did she know more than she was telling me?

I realized after, that I should have asked for George's telephone number, or at the least asked where he was. I had been too preoccupied in sounding casual that I had missed the opportunity. I felt like a moron. That secretary woman had dismissed me with her condescending attitude; moreover I had let her do it. I decided to wait a day before calling her back for the particulars I wanted.

# Chapter 36
# My world is turned upside down.

The next morning I was awakened early in the morning by a loud banging on the door, followed by the ringing of the doorbell. I threw my robe on, and dashed downstairs without putting my slippers on. Each step made me more and more anxious of the urgency of the callers. Had something happened to George? Nervously, I shouted before opening the door.

"Who's there? What do you want?"

"This is the F.B.I. Ma'am, would you be kind enough to open the door and we will show our credentials."

I looked through the peep-hole, and saw two well dressed gentlemen holding their badges up for me to see. Slowly, I held the door ajar and looked around it. I was embarrassed; I was not dressed, and I was nervous that I was in the house alone. The elder man spoke in a gentle voice, and apologized for them knocking so hard on the door.

"I am sorry we alarmed you. Are you Mrs. Daniels?"

I answered them in a shaky voice that I was, but could they explain why they had come to my home. My knees were about to give way so I decided, after checking their badges, to let them in before I fell to the ground in front of them.

I took them through to the lounge, and told them I had to sit down. I asked if they would like to take a seat, but they declined. I had a fierce aching in the pit of my stomach. Anxiety and apprehension constrained me from asking the obvious question. I looked up to them in silence; my nervous eyes were pleading them to explain their visit.

The elder gentleman spoke first.
"We are here to see your husband."

I told him he was not at home at the moment.

"Can you tell us when you expect him back home?"

I knew I couldn't answer his question. I lipped my dry mouth, and bit on my bottom lip before trying to find the right words to explain his absence.

"My husband is working overseas just now, on business. He told me he didn't know when his dealings would be completed, so I am afraid I can't give you an exact date." I answered, trying to be as calm and composed as possible.

"Where exactly is he doing this business?" The younger agent asked in a very officious, firm manner.

I didn't want to admit that I didn't know, and I desperately wanted to stand my ground in front of this authority, so I quickly regained my confidence. I stood up.

"Excuse me Sir, but why precisely have you come to my home to question me, or my husband? I have been out of town myself for a while, and therefore, I am not completly up to date with my husband's affairs. I suggest you ask his secretary for the information you require, or better still, wait until he returns." I said with self-reliance. "Unless of course you could share with me the reason for your visit?" I added with less insistence.

The elder man then told me that their visit was not something they were willing to discuss with me.
"At the moment, our inquiries are particularly centered on your husband, and I feel the matter is something, only he can explain. We will contact his secretary, and hopefully she can assist us. I am

sorry, if I have alarmed you. That was not my intention."

He then gave me his business card, and told me to let him know when my husband returned, or better still, ask him to call the extension number on the card.

They turned to leave, and headed for the front door. I had to ask the apparent question before they left.
"Is my husband in trouble? Serious trouble I mean? Why do you want to speak to him?" I pleaded, addressing my concern to the elder, agent, the kindlier of the two.

He turned to me as he went through the door.
"Don't worry, Mrs. Daniels, I am sure this matter can be explained to our satisfaction when we speak to him. Enjoy the rest of your day."

I closed the door, and rested my body against it, agonizing the reason for the F.B.I. to come looking for George. I needed to speak to my husband, to alert him of their visit, and hopefully he would then explain to me what it might be about.

I went quickly to the telephone, and dialed Glenda's extension, hoping she would be in the office early. It rang and rang and then the infernal answering machine clicked in with the usual instruction to leave a message.

"Glenda, this is Mary. I need to speak to you urgently. You must call me immediately. The F.B.I. has just been here asking for George. I need his contact number, his cell phone is not responding. What is happening?"

I was going into panic mode, and I had to control myself. There was no-one I could call to help me, it was necessary for me to keep it together, and think logically. My body was shaking so I had to calm down. I went to George's drinks cabinet, and poured myself a small whisky, which I swallowed in one gulp.

The taste was not nice, but it did seem to have the right result, and I took a deep long breath, before going into the kitchen to settle my aching stomach with food and a hot drink.

Toast and coffee was all I could muster, my head was spinning with possibilities both big and small, none of which made sense. I had never been in a situation where I was questioned by authority. Even the local police were men and women I had never encountered. The F.B.I. were people I saw on television, so I knew they were more significant than the police. I was frightened to be in this incredible situation with no answers, and no support. Where was my husband?

Just then the telephone rang; it jogged me back to reality. I quickly ran to pick up the receiver. It was, thank God, Glenda on the other end.

"Good morning Mary, I hope you are well? I received your message, and I have been in touch with Mr. Daniels. He noted your concerns, and told me you have nothing to worry about. It is just a passport matter. Apparently, he has lost his passport, and before they can renew it for him to re-enter the States, there are issues to be solved. Simple things I can deal with, nothing for you to worry about unnecessarily; just leave it to me. Oh, by the way if we can solve the matter by Friday, he will be back home Saturday. Take care. Let me know if there is anything else I can do for you." Then, as usual for Glenda the line went dead. I had been dismissed once more.

I called Deering to say I couldn't do any guide work for them for a few weeks because I had some personal problems I must deal with. Actually in retrospect I think I made a mistake by keeping myself out of contact with people. It would have kept me busy, and away from the turmoil.

As the weekend approached I was a complete wreck. I had not heard from George, nor did I have any contact with Glenda. I knew it was reasonable for me to call her again, but somehow I felt uneasy doing so.

"Hallo Glenda, Mary here."

"Yes Mary, I can see it is you from my screen. How can I help?"

The pompous, haughty woman was talking to me like an irritable child. How dare she, I was furious. I responded,

"Ms. Morris you are my husband's secretary, and in that role I asked you to keep me informed as to his schedule and situation. You have failed to do this, therefore when my husband does get back, I will report your lack of performance to him. This is not acceptable Ms. Morris. I need a phone number from you, and some indication of his whereabouts. Now is when I want this from you, do you understand?" It was my turn to sound arrogant and superior.

I think she was rather surprised at my manner, but I was successful in getting a contact number for my husband, and I reciprocated by banging the receiver down without thanking her or giving the usual farewell salutation.

I realized I should think what to say to George before calling him. I didn't want to make a fool of myself if the reason for the F.B.I. visit was only a passport problem. However, the manner of the two agents was rather over the top if that was the only reason for their visit. I decided to be honest and forthright – I would tell George I was confused and frightened by their visit, and then ask him to explain.

I was just about to make that call when my telephone rang, and almost made me jump out of my skin. It was George on the other end, sounding so casual and relaxed. Apparently, Glenda had called him to say I was disturbed and troubled by the visit of the F.B.I. He more or less reiterated the story Glenda had told me, and said it was nothing to alarm myself about.

"When are you coming home, George? I want you here." I said, trying not to sound maudlin.

"As soon as I can sort matters out, dear." He answered in an impatient voice. "Let Glenda know if you require anything, she will take care of the house bills, and anything else you want her to address until I return. Are you O.K. for money?

Just charge everything, that's the easiest way. I will call you tomorrow or the day after, if I have cleared everything up. Take care of yourself, Mary. Love you."

"Love you, get back soon," was the only response I could make.

I sat staring into oblivion, unsure of everything.

JUDY SERVENTI

# Chapter 37
# Falling Apart

The days and weeks that followed the phone call from George are now just a muddled jumble of events. I can't remember clearly which occurrence came first, or in what order they took place. Each one seemed to hit me further down into despair. I could not answer the questions I was being asked, I felt like I had been living in a cocoon unaware of what was going on. Their questions were logical and simple, but my explanations were pathetic.

There was an occasion I received a call from Glenda informing me that the Federal Bureau of Investigations and the United States Department of Treasury had issued a warrant to search George's office and my home, so I was to expect them.

George still had not returned.

I have to say these gentlemen were kind and considerate people. They explained to me that they believed my husband had used his firm to dupe wealthy investors in New York and Florida into buying legal settlements at steep discounts with promises of huge profits; however, his scheme was fiction

In fact, to my horror, I was told that my husband, my George, had been misappropriating funds from investor's trust accounts. As a side investment he sold bogus or non-existent legal settlements. He was robbing Peter to pay Paul.

George still had not returned.

The officers took a lot of files from his home office. I had no idea what they took from his company office, and truthfully, I really did not want to know. They systematically went through every drawer in the house, and made an inventory of everything in the house, as well as our large garage.

They made many visits to the house. I felt purged and slighted on every call. One agent wanted to know where my jewelry was kept, and I told him all my necklaces and earrings were in the box in my dressing table drawer. He didn't believe me. I tried to convince him that I only liked to wear pearls, and the set I had, belonged to me before I was married. He didn't believe me. I desperately needed George to return to support my statements.

He still had not returned.

Then I remembered the expensive jewels George had bought me, and I told the officer how I had asked George to keep them in the office safe, and not in our home.

"Now Mrs. Daniels, tell me where your jewelry is really hidden. All you ladies love to have the trinkets to show off to your friends."

I was livid with this man and responded.

"This lady happens not to like gaudy things, and I am happy with the simple things in life. This pretentious house and everything in it could go up in flames, and I wouldn't care." I began to sob.

"I am sorry," he said leading me gently to the sofa. "I am only doing my job, and in a lot of these cases the culprits hide their ill-gotten gains from us. Or, at least try to."

He sat down beside me, and told me he had done a lot of background checking on George and me. He knew about my volunteering work, and also the fact that I was not seen at many of the social events, or charity functions with my husband. He also tried to console me by adding that anything that was mine and had not been given to me from the company, would not be confiscated. All my own personal belongings were mine to keep. I quietly thanked him, but could not stop shaking.

"Is there anyone I could call to comfort, and help you through this ordeal?" He said with a genuine gesture.

"I have no-one to call. I have no family, and my only true friend is now living in Japan." I answered honestly.

"I could get a woman officer here if you like."

"Thank you, but no. I am sure my husband will be back soon. He probably isn't aware of all this upheaval."

"Oh, but he does, I am sorry to say." The agent assured me.

I couldn't let myself acknowledge that fact, it was inconceivable that my husband would leave me in such a position, accounting for matters I really didn't know about.

Later that day the elderly agent received a call which he shared with me. Apparently George had returned to Miami in a private jet, and had surrended to the police. I had no words to respond to this information, I was bewildered and confused. I just stared blankly into the agent's eyes.

"Personally, I would stay here." He told me, responding to my perplexed manner. "I am sure he will have a good attorney to get him released until a trial date is set, and there is bound to be a lot of media interest, which you don't want to be involved with. I just wish you had someone to stay with you; it won't take long before the reporters arrive on your doorstep. Maybe we could put a police officer outside for your protection, there must be many disgruntled clients looking for your husband, and anything could happen."

He also told me to not answer the telephone, or the door. Before he left he was kind enough to arrange for a woman officer to stay indoors with me, and a male officer to be on duty outside. I felt imprisoned in my own home, I wanted the nightmare to end, but I recognized it was only the beginning of the revulsions to come.

The female officer was a kind and considerate woman who had obviously been in this kind of situation before. She went into the kitchen and made some hot tea, which she brought into the lounge for me. She advised me to take something to help me sleep, and then go to bed and try to rest. I took her advice, and after a lot of tossing and turning my racing mind was dulled by the tablets.

I know I had not been asleep for very long before I was awakened by a commotion outside. I looked through my bedroom window, and saw television trucks, cameramen and reporters with microphones in my driveway. I put on my robe, and went downstairs to find my kind officer.

She explained that maybe there would be something on the television news to explain the crowd outside our home. One part of me was worried for George, but yet another part was resentful he had put us in that terrible position. The officer suggested we put on the television to see if she was right, and then we would know what was going on, and I would be better prepared.

We did, and the fiasco was there for the whole world to see. To my horror I saw George; he was smiling, even though he was handcuffed. He seemed to be enjoying all the attention he was getting from the press who were coaxing him for answers. The pushing and the rough handling of the crowd as he tried to reach the door of the courthouse did not perturb him. He was wallowing in the attention, not at all embarrassed by his situation. I was ashamed at his narcissistic behavior.

Later that unbearable day I was informed that George had been refused bail. Apparently, he was considered a flight risk. His attorneys were not good enough, or maybe his crime was too ruthless, I could only speculate, I had no prior experience to go by. 'Where did this leave me?' was the only question I could ask when I was told by the officer.

"Perhaps you should contact your attorney for the answer. It is very crucial for you at this time to get legal advice." She said with concern.

I didn't like to confess at that time that I had no idea who was George's legal representative. Brad had been the only lawyer I had known, and he was in New York hanging on to life with a thread. I couldn't ask him. I had to call the office, and hope Glenda had some answers for me.

I did just that, but the result was not what I expected. After explaining who I was to the receptionist, she quietly told me that Ms. Morris had been taken into custody that morning, and she had been told to explain, to whoever called, that the office was temporarily closed for business until further notice.

"I suppose I am out of a job, Mrs. Daniels?"

I enlightened her that I was not familiar with the workings of the company, but could she put me through to the office manager. She obliged, and a very nervous voice answered.

He told me about the circumstances I already knew about, and he also informed me that he was afraid he would be next to be summoned by the authorities.

"Is there a legal representative in the office I could speak to?"

"Well, I think they still might be in court, but I will get someone to call you as soon as they return." Then he added. "I'm sorry things had to ….be…..result…..have this outcome." He stuttered on the edge of breaking down, I hope you are O.K."

I answered very briefly, and asked him to be good enough to get the legal department to call me immediately when they returned. I was in no condition to pander to his self-pity, I had to survive this ordeal myself, alone.

# Chapter 38
# Closure

The company attorneys were too busy advising and representing my husband, and his co-conspirators to spend time with me. It wasn't until I finally got to speak to George, to ask for some help, did they reluctantly offer to be of assistance to me.

My conversations with my husband in the weeks and months that followed were very short and strained. I couldn't begin to fathom the why or how behind his escapades. He had hurt so many people, and destroyed so many lives, because of his greed. I was just numb in his company, how could I have been so naive to believe it was just 'good business' that was contributing to our economic situation. I felt duped, so I was very conscious of the anguish coming from his swindled clients.

"They just wanted to get rich fast and big, they knew the chances, they played roulette along with me." Was the way George explained his investors to me, with no repentance.

I lived like a hermit during the pre-trial months. Calling for take-out meals, which I seldom finished, going online for necessary grocery items to be delivered. I was a prisoner in my own home, sinking down into the depths of despair, with no one to call. Barbara was in Japan, and had given me her e-mail address; however, I could not share my grief with her, I was too ashamed.

The media and newspaper reporters bombarded me with calls so many times; as a consequence I pulled my only lifeline out of the socket. When they found out my cell number I was at my wits end, after smashing it to the floor, I stamped on it over and over again, screaming and crying for them to leave me alone. When I had no breath left, my weak body gave way, and I fell to the floor.

I must have blacked out. I have no recollection of the time I had lay there. I awoke with a very bad headache, and an amazing thirst. At first I couldn't move. I could only believe that I had fallen hard on the floor, but luckily I had missed the coffee table. I took my time testing my limbs for mobility before turning over, and with the help of the sofa, I finally stood erect.

I made my way into the kitchen to rinse my face in the kitchen sink, and to put my mouth over the tap to drink. I didn't trust myself to retrieve a glass from the cupboard. I sat at the kitchen table with my head on my arms trying to recover. Slowly my aching head took stock of my predicament. My sense of endurance was slowly overtaking my self-pity. Anger appeared to dampen the dismay in my mind. I went to the bathroom to take a pain killer, and decided I would take a shower to clear my mind and body. Mary Daniels had to face these demons alone.

My husband's trial date arrived, and he hadn't contacted me at all in any way. I was torn between being at his side throughout the trial, or watching it on television, as thousands of other people might be doing. During his prison confinement, while he waited for the trial date, I had been to see him twice. He showed no remorse, nor did he ask me to forgive him for his actions. He truly did not understand, or care about, the backlash effect it had on me. Our conversations were complacent niceties, which held no true value. The man in prison was not the George I had loved and married, but a corrupt, immoral man, who was uncaring, and had no regrets for his actions.

George was inept to be trusted; I was degraded, besmirched to be present at his side. I felt tainted being part of his corruptness, and could not bring myself to appear in court as his supporter.

During the trial he tried to explain to the court that he had expanded his business because he needed more investors' money to fund settlements, and that he had to freeze their trust accounts to appease Florida Bar Regulations. I think he underestimated the Prosecutor who was so obviously part of the Florida Bar, who called him out to the fact that this was a lie.

I cancelled my daily paper, and stopped listening to the news. Then one day a multitude of media, and reporters, again appeared on my doorstep. They shouted out questions, which indicated to me that the trial was over. I switched on the news.

The charges, which were printed out on the screen, were made by the U.S. Securities and Exchange Commision. They alleged - Fraud involving millions in certificates of deposits, and other charges related to the "Racketeer Influence and Corrupt Organisation Act", they were all proven. George, my husband, was a guilty man.

Mrs. Daniels, the wife, wanted to calm him, however, Mary Daniels, the survivor, the injured party, was confounded. I had no words to console him. How could I placate his dealings? His contrition for his many victims was unreal, and shameless. Finally, he was sentenced to 50 years imprisonment. I was never going to share a bed with George again; never would we watch the sun set over Miami from our waterfront patio. Our life together had ended.

The court appointed a receiver to confiscate all George's ill-gotten gains, which included our house, and everything inside. The lists had been made by the F.B.I. agents on their earlier visit, but now came the procedure of taking them away. The agents arrived with three large flatbed trucks, along with six or more removal men wearing overalls with the name "National Liquidators" on the back.

They emptied the large garage of all George's prize vehicles, and the limousine he used daily. The elderly agent who, I had met before consoled me through the ordeal.

He told me to pack my personal belongings, and be sure to watch the men did not take my possessions. I left the turmoil downstairs to go to the sanctuary of our bedroom, and looked around at the contents. None of it was of my choosing; in fact the décor was large and tasteless. Not a picture or an ornament had come from our first home; I had no obligation to keep any of it.

I had to take stock of my circumstances, and think rationally. Where would I go? Our joint bank account had been frozen, and although I did have a little cash, and a personal credit card I had owned since before I was married, that was the sum amount of my assets.

I had a question for the agent, which I went downstairs to ask.

"Excuse me officer, I have a question about this house."

"Of course Mrs. Daniels, what is it?"

"Well, our first house was bought jointly, I was working back then." I struggled to sound logical, but went on.

"When my husband, or the company bought this house, I was not involved, however, I personally did not receive any monies from the sale of our other home. I presume some of it was put into the purchase of this Miami property, so do I get my original investment back?"

He rubbed his fingers around the small stubble on his chin, and then looked directly at me.

"I'm sorry to say, Mrs. Daniels, but I guess you will have to file a claim along with all the other injured parties. I should consult your husband's lawyers on that matter, but all these possessions have to be sold first, before anybody gets anything."

"Thank you." I meekly said as I walked away.
I looked around at all of the activity taking place, and could not comprehend what was happening. Although I had no bond to the things they were removing, I felt an inequitable sense of unfairness that I should be the one to witness this scene. They were literally sweeping the carpet from under my feet, and I was whirling around, not knowing if I could establish myself as the owner of anything.

I wanted to escape the turmoil. The mayhem and confusion was spinning in my head, I knew my mind wanted to shut out the deplorable state of affairs, and I was determined to calm myself, and control the lightheadedness. I sat on the sofa to support my legs, but I could not manage to prevent the tears streaming down my face. The iniquitous, inhuman activity was too much for me to take. 'What had I done to deserve this outcome?' I silently cried.

No one had noticed, or even become aware of my condition, they were all too busy dismantling my home. I ran out of the room, and retreated back to my refuge, my bedroom. I lay on the bed hugging my pillow for the ease of comfort I needed. I sobbed until my body lacked the strength to continue. I had exhausted the will to prolong my agony; I could see no hope, no reconciliation to my dilemma. I had no one to help me, no place to go.

## Chapter 39
## The wide open spaces

I must have eventually fallen asleep through pure exhaustion, because I awoke to the realization that I was not dreaming, the nightmare was for real. There was someone knocking at my bedroom door. I did not want to answer it. A voice I recognized to be that of the sympathetic F.B.I. agent called my name.

"Mrs. Daniels, I'm sorry but we will have to empty your room. Could you collect your belongings, and pack your personal things as soon as possible? The men have only this room to clear."

I looked around in pure dismay. What belonged to me? What was I entitled to take? If I did own anything, I had no place to send it to, no forwarding address. I soon assessed my situation - Mary Daniels was homeless.

I knew I could not carry many things. I went to my closet to retrieve my small suitcase with wheels, which I had purchased when I brought back the brochures and souvenirs from New York, for the pupils of St John's.

I had only one personal, precious belonging I would not leave behind, and that was tucked away at the back of the closet. I carefully retrieved the urn of my one and only child, and placed it in the case, weeping again with the inescapable conclusion of events.

My mind-set then went into a survival mode. I needed essential toiletries. I took a towel and flannel, and wrapped it around the urn. I put in soap, and some small bottles of shampoo and body lotion I had brought from my hotel stays. Finally I decided to put in a roll of toilet paper that I was sure would have many purposes.

One change of clothing, but several pairs of panties, were my next items to pack. The bag was filling up, and I didn't want it to be too heavy. I looked around the room that held no real happy memories for me. What more did I need? My eyes went to my dressing table where I went to sit on the chair, and looked in the mirror. I saw what I felt inside, an empty shell. I had no desire to put on make-up or comb my hair; however, I did put a comb into my purse. I opened the drawer, and saw my reliable set of pearls that had always brought me good luck. I put the case alongside the comb, and closed the clip.

I changed into a pair of jeans and a T-shirt. Also just to be prudent, I put on sensible shoes. I packed a sweater, and put a raincoat over the handle of my wheelie bag. I was ready to leave.

My friendly F.B.I. agent was still outside the door.

"Have you marked the things that belong to you Ma'am? He asked.

"I have everything that is important to me in here." I answered, patting the wheelie bag. I looked up into his surprised eyes. "Goodbye, Sir, I will be off, and out of your way."

"Good luck Mrs. Daniels." I heard him say as I retreated down the stairs in a clumsy fashion.

I walked out of the door, and saw the removal men hoisting my car on to one of the flatbed trucks. I took a deep long breath of fresh air, and walked out of the gate, never looking back.

So it was that I had reached the rock bottom of my life. I was on the streets, not knowing which way to go or where I was heading for. I walked aimlessly along sidepaths, which should have been familiar, it was my neighborhood after all, but I had never consciously noted my surroundings as I drove along in my car.

I looked up at the swaying palm trees lining the sidewalk, and the colorful plants that surrounded the houses. I took another deep breath of the fresh, clean air, which enticed me to think more positively about my situation. George's foibles were never cherished by me, so I shouldn't miss them. I was beginning to realize that I had no regrets. They were taken away, and I didn't want them.

I must have been walking without a true direction for days, I don't really remember as the days and nights merged together. To be safe I was careful to avoid going into the known homeless areas. I suppose that is why I was such an oddity in that vicinity, and attracted such distaste from the public.

It was that day, as I sat on the bench at a bus stop the most unlikely coincident happened. I think I was dozing through fatigue or maybe boredom when I thought I heard an imaginary voice calling my name. Bleary-eyed I looked up, but only saw the cars slowly crawling by, probably anticipating the red light in front of them.

"Mary, Mary Daniels. Is that you?" The voice rang in my ears, as my muddled head tried to focus, but my weary eyes discerned only shapes of passing vehicles, there were no pedestrians around me. I closed my eyes to shut out the illusion, and hoped I was not losing all my faculties as well as my safe habitat.

I think I must have dozed off again, because I dreamt that my Father's strong arm was around me, encouraging me, supporting me. I put my head on his shoulder, and felt his knees against mine.

In my delusionary state I heard a familiar voice whisper in my ear.

"It's O.K. Mary. I am here to help you."

I tried to open my exhausted eyes, and focus on the face, but no recognition came to mind.

I was contented to relax. I felt safe and secure for the first time in ages. The voice spoke again quietly and softly.

"Let me assist you from this bench, Mary and into my car. Please understand I only want you to be safe and out of harm's way. I don't want to rush you, but Mary please try to focus, then you will know who I am."

My muddle state of mind felt swayed by the sincere voice, but the sensible part of me felt vulnerable to strangers. I had to protect myself, and be cautious of unfamiliar people. I pulled away, and moved further along the bench. The man continued speaking to me in a gentle caring voice. He seemed to know a lot about me, so I rubbed my eyes and looked at him more closely.

"You do like your coffee very milky with no sugar Mary Daniels." He said with a more determined voice.

"Terry, is that really you?" I said with conviction.

He smiled and reached for both of my hands. "Let's go." He replied with relief in his voice.

He assisted me the short walk to his car where he wrapped a car rug around me before handing me a bottle of water, which I drank in three large gulps.

Then I felt more awake. However, I was humiliated that he should find me in such an embarrassing situation.

"Terry I am ashamed, I feel so guilty you found me in this situation. I am a wreck; I have nothing, not even hope. I just ….." I rambled on. However, he put his finger across my lips to stop my rantings. Without warning the tears once again flowed down my cheeks. He moved his hands to cup my cheeks, and stared into my watery eyes.

"I admired you before, and my feelings are so much more now that I can hardly contain myself. I know what he did to you Mary. I watched it tirelessly evolve on the screen, for the whole world to see, but I didn't think I would see you again, and especially in these circumstances. Let me help you Mary, even if it is only for today. I can offer you a hot bath, a good meal, and a warm bed for the night, if you would let me." He squeezed both my hands in his, silently, urgently, waiting for my answer.

I couldn't respond. My thoughts were racing in all directions. I couldn't let Terry be dragged into my life; I was the wife of a notorious Ponzi schemer. I was tarnished by my husband's dishonest actions, and maybe I could be held responsible somehow, if the authorities wanted to pursue that course of action.

On the other hand, I was homeless, and I knew my stamina, my funds, and my disposition would not last long.

"Mary, please just come for one day, today, then you can decide what you want to do next. You look totally worn out, and I cannot leave you here. Please, for my sake, if not yours, let me take care of you."

I couldn't answer his plea, my stubbornness; my resolve was clouding my judgment. I could not perceive that his generous offer was the only way out of my situation.

"Why are you being so obstinate, Mary?" He earnestly asked, "Are you frightened of me? I would never harm you. I am sure you know how much I care for you. I cannot, and will not leave you here. You are not thinking logically, you need to be in a safe environment, so you can make rational and sensible decisions on where you want to be. I've a good mind to drive away now, and make the decision for you."

I smiled at his intensity. Yes, for the first time in ages I was happy, smiling and not crying. I squeezed his hands and nodded in response. He smiled as he helped me into his car, and together we headed for his home.

## Chapter 40
## What is a Home?

The day extended to weeks, and the weeks into months and finally on the anniversary of my one year with Terry, I knew where I wanted to be.

My partner, my confidant, saw me through several rough patches. I was called to go for numerous official interviews, and even a deposition which was soul destroying. The authorities grilled me, harassed me, and cojoled me, many times. They did not believe I could have been so naive about George's affairs.

Terry steadfastly stayed loyal to me. We even role-played situations that enabled me to anticipate some of the questions, and then give sincere objective answers. He helped me overcome my fears of officialdom by boosting my self-image. He was my rock.

It was around this time that Terry got offered a job in Upstate New York. He asked me to go with him, and of course this time there was no hesitation from me.

I was eager to escape this city, and all its memories. I would love to be near enough to the metropolis to enjoy my true pleasures. Terry understood clearly what made me happy. In fact I wouldn't have put it past him to have orchestrated the move, but that he wouldn't discuss.

The choosing of our home this time was a far cry from my experience with George. Who, by the way was well out of my system. He had never contacted me, and I was fully complacent with that arrangement.

Terry and I were interested in preservation, with history, and condition was not a major concern, the setting was. His job was very similar to the work he did at Deering, and there were plenty of opportunities for me to do volunteer work alongside him.

We moved together, and found our 'shangri la', a place in the countryside, but near enough to work, and the city of New York. An old house that was full of character, and faults. A place that had witnessed many inhabitants live and die. It was truly a home, not just a house. It oozed warmth and contentment. We both knew the minute we first walked in, it was the place we would find everlasting pleasure together. I had found my safe haven and a sincere soulmate to share it with.

## JUDY SERVENTI

I would never look at a homeless person in the same way, ever again.

Printed in Great Britain
by Amazon.co.uk, Ltd.,
Marston Gate.